MARK *of the* WOLF

A Western

R. Annan

One Vision Publishing

Mark of the Wolf
Copyright 2017 by R. Annan
WGA Reg. #: R32273 (5/15/17)

Editor: Karren Doll Tolliver
Cover Image: Pixabay CCO

One Vision Publishing
Florida, USA
Published 2017
ISBN: 978-1-942338-72-7 (eBook)
ISBN: 978-1-942338-71-0 (Print)

This book is a work of fiction. Any references to real events, businesses and locales are intended only to give the fiction a sense of reality and authenticity. Any resemblance to actual persons, living or dead, is entirely coincidental.

Western books by R. Annan

Fight for the Lazy M
The Red Bandana
The Salvation of Trace Logan
The Cowboy from Sierra Blanca

Jack Cordell Westerns

The Gunfighter in Winter
Long Ride to Hell's Kitchen
Owl Hawks
Gunfight at Barfield Springs
Shootout at Sanctuary City
Last Days of a Gunfighter

Clay Jared Westerns

Copperhead Moon
Cowboys of the Box R
Prisoners of Brimstone Pass
Range War in C Minor
Devil Wind
Showdown at Wamego Falls
Lightning Riders
Winter Kill
Wild River
Shootout at Rattlesnake Flats

Jesse Garnett Westerns

Gunfight at Black Wolf Lair
Gunfight at Latigo Junction
Outcasts of Troublesome Creek
Stagecoach to Bremer's Rock

Dedication

To my daughter Laura

This one is for you, girl!

Chapter 1

Jim Settler was sitting at the desk in his den at the Rafter S Ranch going over some paperwork when his daughter Laura walked in. That's when the argument began again. It was the same argument they had been having for the last three months.

"You'll marry Tobey Nester whether you like it or not!" Settler demanded with authority.

"Well, I won't like it, Father," Laura replied. "I won't like it at all."

A tall, pretty, sturdy girl with long, black hair and piercing green eyes, Laura Settler stared fascinated at the mounted wolf's head on the wall behind her father's desk. Its jaws were wide open in a snarling grimace, showing its large, sharp teeth and angry glare.

"Why don't you like Tobey, honey?" Settler asked, a little less demanding this time.

"Because he smells like dirt, Dad!"

"All farmers smell like dirt, Laura. You'll get used to it," Settler replied. "Look at Mary Templeton. She and young Loren are getting along just fine. She didn't like him at first, but now they've settled down, have two kids and are as happy as two birds in a nest."

"She gave up," Laura insisted. "Mary's parents wore her down." She shivered and stopped staring at the mounted wolf head.

Walking to the den window, she looked out into the yard and saw Marty Parker, the old chuck wagon cook, talking to one of the ranch hands. Parker, once tall, was now bent and weathered from long years of riding the range. Next to her father, Laura loved wise, old Marty the most.

In days gone by, as ramrod of the Rafter S Ranch, Marty had taught her how to ride and shoot. When her mother had died a few years ago, he stepped in to fill the void in her life. He was the only one who could make her laugh. When he got too old to ramrod, her father had hired him on as cook rather than cut him loose to wander around looking for a job.

A new cowboy named Nick Hunter took over as ramrod. He was different than Marty Parker. Whereas Parker was warm and friendly, Hunter was cold and distant. However, he did his job well and that's all that counted. Her father kept Hunter on, but they were never as close as old Marty and her father were. As for Laura, she didn't like Hunter much and avoided him whenever possible.

Her father's voice broke through Laura's thoughts. "Liking Tobey Nester has nothing to do with it," Settler insisted. "It's just how things are done out here. It's for the good of the Rafter S. The ranch comes first. Without it, we're nothing."

Settler figured the marriage between his daughter and the son of farmer Ty Nester would make them the two biggest landowners in a fifty-mile radius. It was for Laura's own good. Jim Settler had no sons to pass the Rafter S Ranch to. So, if Laura married Tobey Nester, she would be secure and her children would inherit a huge cattle and farming empire. Ty Nester and Jim Settler had discussed the matter and come to an understanding that Tobey and Laura would someday marry. It would be beneficial to both families.

"Tobey is coming out here this evening, and, if he makes you an offer of marriage, I'll expect you to accept it."

"Well, if he does, he'll be wasting his time, Dad," the young girl replied stubbornly.

Settler sighed and slammed his hand down on the desk. He had reached the end of his patience. It was to be Tobey Nestor or no one. Laura had frustrated him at every turn. He'd tried to get his daughter to do what was best for the ranch and she'd refused. She had challenged his authority for the last time. The rancher wouldn't tolerate it any more.

"You dare disobey me, girl?" Settler said sternly.

"I will if I have to, Father," Laura replied emphatically. "Mother would never force me to marry someone I didn't love. You know that."

For a moment, Settler was put off, but he quickly went back on the attack. He spoke with authority and force. "Well, your mother isn't here. You will marry Tobey Nester and that's the end of it!"

He saw the hurt on his daughter's face as she turned from him and ran. Her footsteps echoed through the house and across the porch. Settler suddenly regretted being so mean. He sighed and went back to his ledger, trying to concentrate. Moments later, he heard a horse ride out of the yard. He smiled. After an argument, Laura usually took a long ride in the fresh air to cool down. When she came back, she would apologize to him and all would be forgiven.

Settler lost himself in his paperwork, going over debits and credits, expenditures and revenues. Time passed and, by the start of evening, he heard several horses ride into the yard. The rancher got up and walked outside onto the porch to greet his ramrod, Nick Hunter, and three of his men. Hunter saluted Settler. The other three saluted him too, then walked all the horses down to the water trough by the windmill. Settler called Hunter over for a talk.

Hunter had been with the Rafter S for about two years. He drifted in one day looking for a job. Settler was impressed by his handling of the ranch hands and his knowledge of cattle. Although they didn't always see eye to eye, and often had heated arguments, Settler tolerated it. Yet, sometimes it was as if Hunter thought he was the boss of the ranch and Settler often had to remind him who really was in charge.

"How many did the wolves get this time, Hunter?"

"Eleven," Hunter replied. "Mostly old ones. The slow and the weak. The bulls probably kept them away from the heifers and calves."

"That's a lot. The last time it was only five. It seems to be getting worse."

"Well, it ain't my fault, if that's what ya mean."

"No, no, I didn't mean it that way, Hunter," Settler said. They stood looking around the yard, avoiding direct eye contact with each other. Settler asked, "Did you kill any of the wolves?"

"Yeah, two."

"Where?"

"About thirty yards north of the west line shack, by the stream."

"That's odd. They usually don't come in that close," Settler replied.

"Well, I told you we oughta set out some traps," Hunter said flatly "I mentioned that last week."

Settler nodded. "Yeah, I suppose we should. Alright, I'll pick up some traps in Tall Pines the next time I go there."

Hunter said, "The boys think there's a bigger one out there. Far out on the fringe. One as black as coal. They call it the Big Black. They claim it's fast as lightning."

"Is that right?"

"Yeah, and the boys are a little spooked about it," Hunter said.

"Maybe it was a bear instead of a wolf."

"I think they'd know the difference," Hunter said defensively.

"Well, next time you go out, find it. Whatever it is, find it and kill it."

"Yeah, I'll do that," Hunter replied dryly. He didn't like being told what to do. Without another word, he headed for the bunkhouse.

Settler walked back into the house to the den and sat down at his desk. He rolled a cigarette and began to think about the wolves. They were becoming a big problem. Hunter's tale about the Big Black was troubling. Settler had already heard stories from some of the smaller ranchers. The story going around was that the Big Black weighed about 200 pounds and had blazing green eyes.

Settler laughed to himself. He didn't believe in such stories. He took them to be tall tales told around the campfires by drunken cowboys. Cowboys liked to exaggerate, especially when they were under the influence of whiskey. The biggest wolf his men had ever killed had weighed about 160 pounds. A two-hundred-pound wolf, if not impossible, was at least unnatural.

He finished his cigarette and went back to his paperwork, wondering when Laura would come back. He began to worry.

Chapter 2

It was late afternoon and the sun was heading west in a cold November sky. Wolves were howling in the hills and long shadows were falling across the land. Laura Settler had gotten over the fight with her father and was returning home after a long ride. About twenty miles from the Rafter S Ranch something startled her horse. The small, dun-colored animal whinnied hard, reared straight up and pawed the air. Caught by surprise, Laura was tossed backwards from her saddle. She came down hard, hitting the back of her head on the ground.

For a while she lay still and helpless where she had fallen. Bruised and shaken, she struggled to her feet and stood looking around on unsteady legs, trying to focus her vision. The air seemed unusually bright and hazy. She put her hand down to her holster only to find her gun had come loose and was lost somewhere in the tall buffalo grass. Her hat had sailed away on the wind.

A stand of silver aspens stood at the edge of a field far to her front. It seemed to whisper and nod to her. She headed that way on weakening legs. The back of her head throbbed where she had struck it hard on the ground. When she finally reached the trees, she noticed how the westering sun danced off the dry leaves, making them sparkle in the waning autumn light. They gave off delicate, tinkling sounds as the wind played amongst them. It sounded to her like strange harp music.

As she stood there, hypnotized by the sights and sounds of nature, she had the uncomfortable sensation that someone or something close by was watching her.

Feeling as if she were in a dream, Laura made her way slowly to the other side of the woods. When she got there, she stopped to rest. In front of her lay another wide field of high, golden-topped broom sedge that stirred in the wind like waves on a sea. She stood scanning it to see if her horse had left a trail there but saw no sign that it had. Finally, heaving a deep sigh, Laura staggered into the field and made her way across. Her legs grew weaker with each step. Halfway to the other side, her skin began to tingle. It wasn't from the cold, but from an eerie feeling that she was being stalked as prey.

There was a sudden swishing sound behind her. Laura stopped and turned. The tall grasses a dozen yards away whipped about violently. She caught the flash of low, grey, sleek forms as they rushed in her direction. It took all her strength to turn and get moving again. Her legs felt too heavy to lift. The frigid air burned her lungs as she struggled towards a stand of pines at the far end of the field. Just when she thought she would make it, a huge, grey wolf leaped high in her direction. Its jaws opened and closed on her right arm, dragging her down into the tall grass. She screamed in pain as sharp teeth pierced her flesh.

At that moment, when she thought she was about to die a horrible death, something strange happened. A huge, black shadow fell over her. She couldn't tell what it belonged to, human or beast. The wolf released her arm, crept back and began to cower and whine. The other wolves turned, too, and went slinking away into the field. They quickly disappeared.

Laura tried to get up, but was too weak. A wave of nausea swept over her, and she fell backwards. Her arm burned and throbbed and was wet where the blood ran down inside her shirt sleeve. The beast's fangs had penetrated deep. Suddenly she felt herself being lifted and carried. The world spun around her as someone or something carried her into the trees and laid her on a bed of soft pine boughs. Before she fainted, she smelled the odor of wolves.

Chapter 3

Tobey Nester came to call on Laura. Her father seated the young farmer at the kitchen table. Over a cup of coffee, Settler explained that Laura had taken her horse for a ride and should be returning any minute now. They made small talk about the weather, cattle, corn prices and other mundane subjects.

"How's your father doing, Tobey?" Jim Settler finally asked when he couldn't think of anything else to say to keep the conversation alive. The older man and the younger boy really didn't have very much in common to talk about.

"Just fine, sir," was all young Nester said and let it hang there.

Laura's father felt a little uncomfortable facing Tobey Nester alone. The truth was he really didn't like the young man. His demand that Laura marry Nester was purely a business arrangement based on projected advantages and not much else. Right now, he wished Laura would come back and take up the slack.

After an hour had passed, Nester got noticeably irritated. He began to look out the kitchen window into the yard for any visible sign of Laura. There was none. Finally, Settler and the young man went out on the porch and sat there smoking and making occasional remarks that they both knew sounded stupid and ill informed. With the sun hovering just above the tree line, Tobey Nester had had enough.

He got up and nodded to Laura's father. "I guess I'll be going now, Mr. Settler," Tobey said. He uttered not one word about being worried over Laura not returning. He said nothing at all to show any concern for her safety and well-being.

"Alright, Tobey," Settler replied dryly. "I'll tell her you stopped by. Give my regards to your mom and dad."

Young Nester touched the brim of his hat in a casual salute and ambled casually down the porch steps to his horse. Mounting up, he rode off toward his family's farm. Jim Settler watched until the young man finally disappeared out of sight behind a rise in the road. He sighed. It hadn't gone very well.

Just as Settler turned to go back into the house he heard horses coming across the field behind the bunkhouse. It was

Tom Rogers, one of the two cowhands who were stationed at the west line shack with Mel Madden. He held the reins of Laura's horse and was towing it behind him. As soon as Jim Settler saw the empty saddle his heart began pounding rapidly. He rushed to meet Rogers with a sober look on his face.

"I found Miss Laura's pony a-wanderin' around out in the west sector, Mr. Settler," the cowhand said with concern. "Madden and me, we searched the area fer miles but didn't see hide nor hair of her."

Settler nodded and took the horse's reins from the cowboy. His heart pounded and he held back a groan, trying to appear stable and in control, even though he was near the edge of panic.

"Alright, Tom," Settler said. "Thank you. You can sleep in the bunkhouse tonight and go back out in the morning. Send Hunter out. I need to talk to him."

Rogers dismounted and walked his horse wearily over to the bunkhouse. He tied it to the hitching rail and went inside. A few moments later, Hunter walked out.

"Tom told me, boss," the big ramrod said. "Whatta ya want me to do?"

"Do? You know what to do!" the rancher yelled, his voice cracking. "You have to go look for her, you fool!"

The ramrod shrugged. He was seeing Settler crack under the strain. The rancher needed him now more than ever. Hunter knew the power was in his hands.

"Sure, Mr. Settler," Hunter said. "Leave it to me. I'll get the boys together an' we'll figure out what ta do."

With that said, Hunter shouted into the bunkhouse. Seconds later seven cowboys came out in a hurry. Some were half-dressed, and one or two had had a little too much to drink. They gathered around Hunter and the rancher.

"Listen up, men," Hunter said, talking very loudly in a pumped-up, authoritative manner. "Miss Laura is out there somewhere all alone on foot. We have to find her before the wolves get to her." Hunter heard Settler wince when he mentioned the wolves. The ramrod suppressed the urge to smile. He wanted Settler to feel pain. This was as good a way as any to do it and get away with it. "If we don't find her in the next five hours, it most likely will be all over fer her."

Settler groaned, "Oh, dear God!"

"What're we gonna do?" one of the cowboys asked. "It's darker than a well digger's behind out there!"

"Not only thet, but it's colder than a witch's tit, too!" one of the drunken cowhands pointed out.

The others nodded. It had gotten noticeably colder and threatened snow. Settler stared pleadingly at Hunter.

"We can't do anything now," one of the cowboys remarked. "Hell, it's too dark."

Hunter puffed up his chest. "One thing we can do is build a signal fire." He pointed to three of the cowhands. "You three, go gather up some wood. The rest of you saddle up yer broncs."

There was some grumbling amongst the remaining men. "Hell," one said, "thet's crazy. There's wolves out there."

"We'll take torches," Hunter countered.

"Thet's even crazier," another yelled. "If we set a fire accidently, Miss Laura could get hurt real bad!"

Hunter saw the folly of a night search and nodded. "Alright, but nobody goes back into the bunkhouse. Get your coats and stand by to help keep the fire going."

Jim Settler felt a little better about the situation now that Hunter had swung into action. After taking care of Laura's horse, he helped with constructing a pyramid of dried wood and branches. Once it was lit and the flames were stretching skyward, he relaxed a little. The cowboys soon were in a jovial mood, and Marty Parker got out his mouth harp and began playing some tunes from long ago. Hunter turned his back on the drinking. Soon a few of the cowhands were dancing around the fire to the tune of what came close to sounding like "The Old Chisholm Trail".

As the night stretched on, chairs were brought out of the bunkhouse and the cowhands crowded around the huge fire to keep warm. Parker loaded up the range stove and heated up a pot of steaming coffee. He served up some leftover biscuits with sorghum molasses. Things settled down and they began telling stories. Some were about horses, some about cattle, and some about women they had known in the past. When an owl hooted in a nearby tree, ghost stories came up. Old Parker was good at that and soon had their ears. His voice rose and fell in cadence with the story at hand. An ambience of eeriness soon set it. One thing a cowboy believed in was spirits and ghosts.

A wolf howled. Parker went slack-jawed and his words drifted down to a whisper.

"Thet's mighty close," a cowboy said. "Darn close."

"Yeah, it sounded like it came from behind the barn," one of the cowboys muttered.

They all stood up slowly and drew their guns, waiting and listening for the next howl that would reveal the location of the animal. A stiff wind shot across the yard and sent sparks dancing and spiraling skyward. The huge fire began to crackle and sink in on itself.

"There it is!" someone yelled and fired a shot into the darkness.

"No! Hold it!" Settler bellowed as he ran towards the open space alongside the barn and the windmill. He disappeared into the deep shadows. Everyone froze with their guns pointed at the spot he had disappeared.

"Mr. Settler! Are you alright?" Parker yelled.

Settler's voice hollered back. "Yes. Don't anybody shoot!"

Jim Settler stepped out from the darkness with his daughter Laura's limp body in his arms.

Chapter 4

When Settler asked how Laura was doing, Dr. Morris Cutter shook his shaggy head and replied, "Not so good, Jim. Not so good at all. She's lost a lot a blood and she's half out of her mind. And she keeps mumbling nonsense about wolves. A lot of gibberish that makes no sense as far as I can figure out."

Jim Settler wasn't sure Morris Cutter was a real doctor or not, but he was the only one in Tall Pines, the nearest town, ten miles away.

"What kind of gibberish, Doc?"

"As far as I kin make out, it's about wolves talking to her and telling her stories and her getting a ride home on a wolf. The craziest stuff I've ever heard." Old Doc Cutter laughed, then quickly turned serious. "A funny thing, though, Jim..." He left the sentence unfinished.

"What's that, Doc?" Settler asked.

The old man took a sip of coffee and shifted in his chair. He looked across the kitchen table at the rancher. "Her fancy trousers, them jodhpurs and coat, they're covered with animal hairs. It's as if she was laying or sitting in a pile of it." He watched Settler's face to see the effect of those words.

"That's odd," was all the rancher could think of saying. He raised his eyebrows and shrugged. "I never noticed that. Anything else, Doc?"

"Well, it looks like her wound was cleaned. By now it should have been infected. It was well attended to, but in a different way."

"A different way?"

"Yeah, there's something odd that I can't explain."

The rancher sat quietly trying to make sense of what the doctor was saying. Laura's feverish ravings and the doctor's words crazily suggested that a wolf had cleaned Laura's wound and brought her back to the ranch. Of course, this was preposterous. To assume that it did happen was insane!

The only way to get at the truth was to talk directly to Laura. "Is she coherent, Doc? Can I talk to her?"

"Ah, no, not right now, Jim."

"Why not?"

"I had to give her a pretty heavy dose of laudanum to settle her down. I'd give her another day, or maybe two," the doctor advised. "You might wanna have someone attend to her. She'll need a woman's help for a while."

Settler nodded, then asked, "Do you happen to know of someone I could hire to stay here and attend to her?"

The doctor seemed to have the answer ready and replied, "There's Toothless Mary, an old Indian woman who lives by herself on the outskirts of town. She does that kind of thing."

"An Indian?" Settler asked scornfully.

"Yeah. An old Comanche. People in town use her sometimes. Nobody has ever complained, as I know of. I hear she charges two bits a day."

The rancher gave out a big sigh of resignation. "Alright. I guess I don't have much choice. I'll send one of the boys in with a buckboard to get her."

"No need. She has an old broken-down pinto she rides. I'll talk to her."

"Could you make it quick, Doc?" Settler asked. "I've got my hands full with the ranch."

"Sure. I'll have her out her sometime today, Jim."

"Thanks, Doc," the rancher said. Then, "Say, did you notice those faint marks on Laura's forehead?"

"Yes, I did. I was going to ask you about them, Jim. When did that happen?"

"She came back with them, Doc. I didn't notice them until I brushed the hair from her eyes. The markin's are real faint."

"They look like four blue upside-down teardrops, don't they?"

"Yeah, that's right, they do, now that you mention it. I tried to wipe them off but they seem to be in the skin. Some sort of dye."

The doctor shrugged. "They'll wear off in time, I imagine. I wouldn't worry about it, as long as she's alright. Oh, by the way, Jim, you won't be seein' me anymore."

"Whatta ya mean, Doc?"

"I'm retiring, Jim, going back to Chicago. I ain't as sturdy as I used to be. It's getting to be a little too much for me out here now."

"Gosh, Doc, I don't know what the valley is gonna do without you."

"You all will do jest fine. The town council has arranged fer a replacement, so don't worry. You'll all be jest fine, jest fine."

When the doctor left, Settler walked upstairs. He stood by the door of his daughter's room for a moment and listened. The big house made sounds, and he could hear the groaning of joists and creaking of timbers as the house contracted in the cold air. Turning the knob and opening the door, he walked slowly inside. He didn't see Laura buried under the bed covers, but then he heard the sound of heavy breathing as she lay in a laudanum induced sleep. One of her hands hung over the side of the bed. Settler walked over, and gently placed it back under the covers.

The rancher stood silently staring down at his daughter's pale face. There were dark circles around her eyes. She looked older than before and yet, at the same time, more innocent and helpless. The big man clenched his fists and shut his eyes as he silently sobbed. Laura was the virtual image of her mother, Rachel. She had been taken away from him by the prairie sickness, and now his only child, Laura, lay stricken before him as well.

His eyes fastened on the strange markings on her forehead, above her eyes. Like the doctor had said, they looked like faded, blue, upside-down teardrops. The two in the center of her forehead were higher, and had a longer stem than the others on its flanks. The stem of those on the flanks pointed inward towards each other. They almost looked like some sort of a hex sign. Settler wondered how they got there. No one would notice them under a hat.

Walking slowly and cautiously backwards to the door, he turned and went downstairs into the kitchen. He looked around. It seemed empty without Laura working at the stove. Towards the end, before Rachel had passed on, Laura was at a finishing school for girls in Chicago. Then, when her mother died, she rushed home to be at her father's side. From then on, she refused to go back to Chicago and, hard as he tried, he couldn't force her to leave the ranch.

Settler poured a cup of coffee, went outside and stood on the porch. When he saw one of the cowboys coming up from the corral, he waved him over and told him to go find Hunter. Five minutes later the big ramrod came up from the barn.

"What is it, boss?" the big ramrod asked impatiently, as if he had been doing something important and was in a hurry to get back to whatever it was.

The rancher looked hard at his ramrod and said, "Those wolves…"

"What about them?"

"It's about time you took them serious, Hunter."

"Me?"

"You're the ramrod around here, aren't you?"

In Hunter's mind, it sounded as if he were being blamed for what happened to Settler's daughter. "Alright, how serious do you figure I should get?"

"More than you have been," the rancher replied sharply. "Like wiping them out. Every last one. Females, males and cubs. The whole darned pack."

Hunter reflected on that for a moment. "That might take some doing."

"I don't care what it takes. Just get it done."

"I'll have to pick the right men out for the job."

"Then do it."

"Sure, I'll do it," Hunter said flatly.

"Get on it now, Hunter! I want those wolves gone as soon as possible."

"Whatever you say, boss." There was sarcasm in Hunter's tone.

Settler turned and walked back into the house. The ramrod turned and walked back towards the barn. "To hell with you, boss," he muttered to himself. "To hell with you." The rancher's superior, patronizing attitude always got to him. Hunter didn't like being talked down to. Not from Jim Settler or anybody else. No, he'd be patient and wait. His day would come, and, when it did, he'd make Settler sorry for the way he treated him.

Back in the bunkhouse the cowboys had heard the exchange between Hunter and the rancher.

"Damn," one of them remarked. "Settler sure got on Hunter's back, didn't he?"

"Yeah," another replied. "But Settler better go easy with Hunter. He ain't nobody ta mess with."

"It's them darn wolves," another said. "They've got everybody all riled up."

As if to emphasize those words, the wolves howled in the hills beyond the barn.

Chapter 5

Hunter assembled a special squad of four men whose sole job was to eliminate the pack of wolves. They were Bundy, Swift, Ford and Teller. Sam Bundy, a short, stocky cowboy with freckles and red hair, was in charge. He had a cheery outlook on life. Originally from Virginia, he had hunted as a boy and was an excellent shot. Rand Swift once tracked renegade Indians for the War Department. Ned Ford and Rod Teller were crack shots with rifles.

Hunter assembled them in the bunkhouse to go over the plan. They sat on a bunk while Hunter stood facing them.

"Boys," Hunter said, "Mr. Settler wants the wolves gone and he's gonna pay you all five dollars a month extra to do it. No more bustin' yer butts wranglin' cows and broncs." He nodded to Bundy. "Sam, tell the boys how you're gonna handle this."

Sam Bundy stood up to speak. He adjusted his gunbelt, sniffed and ran a finger under his nose. That done, he puffed his chest up like a rooster and spoke. "Since most of the wolves are operatin' in the west sector, that's where were gonna be hangin' out. We'll go out there an' hunt 'em down until we kill every last one of 'em."

"Won't we need a huntin' dog?" Rand Swift asked. "Seems like it'd be easier if we had us a huntin' dog."

That caught Bundy off balance. He looked over at Hunter for help.

"Forget about dogs. There ain't gonna be no dogs," Hunter said. "It's just the four of you out there killing wolves.

"About Miss Laura," Ford said. "How is she doin'?"

"I don't know," Hunter replied indifferently. "Settler doesn't talk about her and I didn't ask."

Ned Ford spouted, "Hell, I reckon he's more worried about the cattle than he is Miss Laura." A second later he realized he'd spoken out of turn and tried to cover up by saying, "Then, maybe not."

"You got a big mouth, Ford," Rod Teller said. "You take thet back or I'll kick yer skinny ass."

Ford shot back with, "You an' what army, Teller? If you feel like a frog, well jest you go ahead an' jump!"

"You need a good ass-whippin', Ford," Swift yelled. "Thet's what you need!"

"Well, jest you come on then, Swift," Ford shot back. "Any time ya want, I'm ready!"

Hunter yelled, "Alright, enough of that crap! If you two can't get along then both of you can hit the trail!" That settled them down. "Alright, then," Hunter continued, "I want you all packed and ready ta go in the morning at sunup. I'll tell Mr. Settler it's done, that he won't have to worry about the wolves anymore."

Sam Bundy nodded. "Thet's right, boss. Give us a week or two, maybe three at most and they'll all be gone," he said boastfully.

Bundy couldn't believe his luck. What a sweet deal this was. They might be able to stretch it out for months, collecting extra pay and just sitting around playing cards and drinking red eye. They might even be able to sneak into town to see the painted ladies from time to time.

Hunter said, "I'll expect you boys to come back once every week with a load of wolf skins on a pack horse. Now, don't disappoint me."

"Don't worry, boss," Bundy said, smiling, "we'll get it done." After Hunter left the bunkhouse to tell Settler he no longer had to worry about the wolves, Bundy sneered, "All he does is strut around an' give orders."

"Yeah," Swift agreed, "he sure don't git his hands dirty, does he?"

Ford laughed, "Why don't you tell him thet to his face, Swift? I'm sure he'd like ta hear it."

"Why don't you tell him what I said, Ford?" Swift shot back.

"Maybe I will," Ford replied in a superior voice. "I jest might do thet."

"An' I'll kick yer butt if ya do," Swift threatened, going after Ford.

Bundy jumped in between the two. "You damn idjits! Stop yer fightin'. Can't ya see what a good deal this is gonna be? We get Hunter off our backs fer a month an' maybe even longer. All we gotta do is drag this thing out."

"Sure, but what about the wolves?" Ford asked. "Hunter will expect we do some killin'."

The mention of wolves sobered them a bit. Bundy and Swift began rolling cigarettes. Ford walked over to his cot and got a pint of whiskey from a wooden crate beneath it. He brought it back and sat down next to Teller, offering him first swig. Teller nodded, took a pull and handed it to Bundy. He, too, took a drink and passed it to Swift. After Swift took a long drink, he handed it back to Ford.

"They say there's something big out there in the west sector," Teller said.

"Yeah, I heard thet, too," Swift replied.

"It's most likely a bear," Bundy said.

"Bears an' wolves don't mix," Ford said. "Were ya find wolves ya won't find a bear within ten miles."

"Well, whatever it is, we're gonna kill it," Bundy boasted.

Though no one said it, they all suddenly felt the need to get courage from the bottle.

Chapter 6

Toothless Mary, the ancient Comanche woman, rode slowly into the Rafter S Ranch yard in the middle of the morning on her brightly painted pinto. She sat on a blanket without a saddle, and held a crude rope hackamore instead of a set of reins. A rawhide pouch hung from a strap that crossed over her right shoulder to her left hip.

Her small, sturdy body was dressed in colorful native clothes. Many necklaces, adorned with animal teeth, bird claws, seeds and painted river rocks, hung around her neck. Her head hung forward on sloping shoulders, and her brown face was flat with skin like the bark of a tree. Mary's face was far from pretty, but it had character. Most notable were her wide cheekbones, long black hair that hung down her back, and her large, deep set, all-seeing eyes. It was also obvious she had no teeth, which caused her mouth to pucker. Her lower lip stuck out more than the top one. This gave her a proud, pouting, stubborn look, which was true to her nature.

Settler met Toothless Mary in the yard and looked her over. In his mind, she was a disappointment. Judging from what she looked like, he doubted she would be of any help. He immediately regretted agreeing to Doc Cutter's suggestion of having her tend to Laura. He was about to send her back to town when Hunter came rushing up to him. The big ramrod had a worried look on his face.

"Can I speak to you, sir?" Hunter asked. He sounded urgent. He glanced at Toothless Mary for a moment, then quickly disregarded her.

"Can't it wait a while, Hunter?" Settler complained. It annoyed him to be interrupted.

"It's pretty important, sir," the ramrod replied.

"Alright, what is it?" Settler asked. They walked a few feet further down the yard, away from Toothless Mary.

"Crawford and Stoner up and quit this morning, sir."

"Crawford and Stoner?"

"Yep."

"Did they say why?"

"They got spooked about this big wolf story that's been goin' around. I tried to explain how you were taking care of it with Bundy and some of the boys, but they wouldn't listen. They said maybe they'd come back when the wolf problem blows over."

"I see," Settler said solemnly. "Have any of the other men left?"

"Not yet. Just them two so far. But I suspect there might be more."

"Well, you'd better figure something out, Hunter. We can't lose any more men at a time like this."

Hunter scratched his chin and pretended to think deep thoughts. "We could offer them a five dollar a month raise, if it comes to that, boss."

The rancher wasn't happy with that solution and replied, "Is that all you can come up with? Figure out something else. And make sure no one else leaves."

"I'll do my best, sir," Hunter replied and quickly left. Settler didn't see the resentful smirk on his face.

He turned around to talk to Toothless Mary, but she was gone. Her horse was tied to the rail by the porch, but she was nowhere in sight. Suddenly it struck him that she might be in the house. Rushing to the porch, Settler hurried inside. In the hall, he could hear a voice upstairs. His heart began to pump hard again as it usually did when he was confronted with fear. He rushed up the stairs, and moments later found himself standing in the open doorway to his daughter's room looking on in horror.

Toothless Mary was hovering over Laura's still form, uttering Comanche incantations. In her left hand, she held a rattlesnake rattle while in her right hand she sprinkled a dusty, vaporous blue powder over the bed.

"Oh, my God! Get away from her, you heathen devil!" the rancher bellowed as he rushed at the Indian woman.

As he came closer, she tossed a handful of powder into his eyes, blinding him. He came to a halt and batted the stuff away, blinking, sneezing and staggering until he tripped over a chair. After that, he drifted off into a half-dream state. From his place on the floor he watched helplessly as Toothless Mary droned on in a deep, moaning voice, waving her rattle, and moving her moccasin covered feet in a series of dance steps that sounded like someone shuffling in the sand. He tried to rise up and get his hands on her throat, but each time he fell back. All he could do was sit and watch.

When she finished the ceremony, Settler felt Toothless Mary take his hand and speak to him in what he thought was

Comanche. The strange thing was, he understood the meaning of her words, then stood up and followed her down into the kitchen. She sat him in a chair and went to work over the stove, brewing a foul-smelling tea. She poured some tea into a tin cup and she went upstairs, leaving him alone.

Later, she returned to the kitchen carrying an empty cup. She refilled it again with tea, and gave it to Settler to drink. It was bitter stuff, but he drank it all and fell asleep over the kitchen table.

When Settler awoke it was dark. Toothless Mary was standing by the stove smoking a long, thin, brown, handmade cheroot. The smoke had a sweet scent to it. She stared at Settler with a smile and nodded through a cloud of smoke.

"Laura!" he yelled. "Oh, God!"

The rancher groaned, jumped up out of his chair, and rushed upstairs to his daughter's bedroom. When he got there he caught the sweet, pungent smell of sage. He saw a small clay dish on the table by Laura's bed. It had little scented sticks smoldering in it. Their ends glowed and sent up curls of aromatic smoke.

Settler walked over to the bed and stood looking down at his daughter. Laura lay relaxed, breathing deeply. She had a content look on her face, and the bloom was back on her cheeks. He watched her for a while. She sighed several times in her sleep. The rancher nodded and went back downstairs.

Evidently, Toothless Mary wasn't just a dumb Indian after all.

Chapter 7

The wolf hunters seemed to be cursed from the beginning. Bad omens began to appear, as signs of what was to come. Annoying problems cropped up, like Ford's horse needing a shoe. He refused to get a different horse from the remuda although there were plenty to choose from. He insisted he wasn't going to put his saddle on any of those cold-backed sons of Satan. "No, sir, not no how, not no way!" Getting Ford's horse re-shoed was the first delay.

Next came the packhorse not being packed correctly. The supplies mysteriously spilled out of the bottom of the pack and it had to be mended. One thing after another occurred to hold them back. It was almost as if fate were toying with them or someone had sent them a curse. On the other hand, maybe fate was telling them not to go. If that was the case, none of them had the foresight to consider that possibility.

When, in the middle of the afternoon, they finally started out on their journey, the weather itself turned against them.

The temperature dropped sharply and the November wind howled at them like a crazed banshee. Hunched over, they held onto their saddle horns in an effort to stay upright. The horses dropped their heads to protect their eyes from flying leaves and branches.

They were about five miles out from the ranch house when Ford, who had stowed several pints of whiskey in his saddlebag, pulled one out and started drinking. Swift and Teller joined in with their own bottles. By the time they reached the west line shack several hours later, all three were in an alcohol induced state of silliness. Bundy soon found he had very little control.

As they came into the flat area where the line shack stood, they noticed that the door was open and swinging freely in the wind. Bundy dismounted and went cautiously inside. He expected to see two cowhands holding down the fort, but there was no sign of them or their horses. There was no fire in the makeshift stone hearth, either, and the ashes were cold. As the others came in, Bundy lit the oil lamp on the table.

"Where the heck are Rogers and Madden?" Teller asked as he tried to focus his whiskey-sodden eyes. He was unsteady on his feet.

"Good question," Bundy replied. "From the looks of it, there ain't been nobody here in the last day or two."

"Maybe they're takin' strays down range so the wolves don't git 'em." Swift suggested. His voice was thick from drinking whiskey. He shook his head to clear it.

"Thet could be," Bundy replied. "But, with the door open like thet, it looks like they might a-left in a big hurry."

A chorus of wolves started howling. They weren't very far away.

Ford smirked at Swift. "They sure sound hungry, don't they, Swift," he laughed, slurring his words. "Better watch out. They'll be a-comin' fer yer big, fat rump ta night."

Teller looked at Swift with a big grin on his face and said, "You gonna let Ford git away with thet, Swift? Kick his ass." He wanted to see Swift and Ford go at each other.

Swift leered angrily at Ford and growled, "Shut yer big yap, Ford, thet ain't nothin' ta joke about."

Ford chuckled. "Yup, they're gonna come fer you, Swift, ol' pal. Right about midnight they're gonna come fer thet big rump a yers. Haw!"

"Alright, Ford, that's enough!" Bundy growled. "Get yer butt out there and find some wood fer the fire. It's gonna be gettin' mighty cold by the time it gets dark an' thet ain't far away."

"Hell, I ain't goin' out there alone," Ford sulked. "There's no tellin' what's waitin' out there."

"Alright. Swift, you go with him," Bundy demanded.

Swift sneered. "Hell, I ain't goin' no place with Ford. He kin kiss my behind!"

"Alright. Teller, you go with Ford an' git some wood, then," Bundy said. "Otherwise we're gonna eat jerky and hardtack an' freeze all the while were here.

"Let him go by himself," Teller said. He could hardly stand on his feet. "I'm gonna take a nap."

Bundy grabbed the front of Teller's coat, pulled him close and glared into his eyes. "You want yer butt kicked, Teller?"

Teller shook his head. He knew the husky little redhead could beat him in a fight, so he smiled. "Okay, Sam, okay." Bundy released the hold on Teller's coat, and Teller staggered towards the door. "C'mon, Ford, let's go git some wood fer the warden. Haw!"

"Hurry it up," Bundy said in a friendlier voice, "it's getting dark. The sooner ya bring the wood in, the quicker we kin make some coffee an' heat up some beans."

Teller and Ford pulled their coat collars up and their hats down lower on their heads. Ford gave Bundy and Swift a sour look then hurried outside with Teller.

"Jesus," Bundy muttered, "here I am stuck with a bunch of drunks. What the hell did I do to deserve this?" He sighed, looked around and said, "C'mon, Swift, let's go bring in the supplies."

Bundy and Swift stepped outside into the yard. The howling of the wolves seemed louder and closer. The horses fidgeted and strained at the rail. Bundy tied the reins tighter. He didn't see Teller or Ford, but could hear them in the nearby trees gathering wood. Suddenly both men began firing off their guns and howling loudly back at the wolves.

Swift remarked cynically, "Jesus, they're both crazy as coyotes."

"I hope the damn fools don't shoot themselves," Bundy replied dryly.

After he and Swift finished getting the supplies, they stayed inside the shack. Ford finally came in with an armful of wood and dumped it carelessly into the empty wood box.

"Teller kin bring the rest," Ford said. He knelt and started placing twigs under the grate in the hearth. "I'll need some paper," he mumbled as he worked.

Swift sat down on a chair next to Bundy at the table. For a moment, he listened to the howling of the wind. It blended with the howling of the wolves and the sound of Teller, outside, howling back at them.

"Damn wolves," Swift muttered with a whiskey-sodden voice.

"Teller sure is a-givin' it back ta them," Ford chuckled.

"We'll fix 'em good tomorrow," Bundy said confidently, sneering. "When we're finished with 'em they won't feel like howlin' anymore."

He nodded as if to assure himself that it would happen. Sitting at the table across from Swift, Bundy watched him try to roll a cigarette with fingers that wouldn't do what they were supposed to do. Tobacco spilled on the table. Swift laughed at his own clumsiness.

"Here," Bundy said and took the paper and tobacco pouch away from Swift. He rolled two cigarettes, put one in his mouth and handed the other to Swift. Once Swift got it in his mouth, Bundy lit them both.

Swift inhaled deeply and blew a plume of smoke into the cold air. "This is a lousy deal," he said, sounding a bit sober. "I got a girl waitin' in town."

"Who ain't?" Bundy replied. He shoved his hands in his coat pockets to warm them. "I forgot my darn gloves."

Swift only nodded and looked through glazed, half closed eyes. He looked like he was about to fall asleep.

Bundy noticed an old, dog-eared pulp magazine lying on the table. He picked it up and flipped through the few pages that were left. When he came to an artist's rendition of a huge wolf attacking a man, he stopped to stare at it. He stared a long time. Somehow, it made him feel uncomfortable, even though it was just a drawing. Suddenly he tossed the magazine over to Ford. It hit him on the shoulder. "There's yer damn paper, Ford."

"Thanks," Ford said sarcastically, picking the magazine up.

He tore several pages out, stuffed them under the wood in the fireplace and lit them. The paper was old and dry and flared up almost instantly. Soon the flames were snapping, crackling and roaring. The fire's glowing warmth quickly spread throughout the shack.

Bundy got a coffee pot and a frying pan from the pile of provisions. He handed the coffee pot to Swift.

"Go fill this up," he said. "An' bring Teller back with you."

"Sure," Swift said. "Make extra beans, will ya? I'm really hungry." With that, he walked outside on wobbling legs and headed for the stream behind the shack.

A few minutes after Swift left, Bundy became aware that the wolves had stopped howling and Teller had stopped howling and shooting, as well. Now all Bundy could hear was the wind as it blew around the corners of the shack. He listened for a moment, shrugged and went to work opening two cans of beans. Dumping them into the frying pan, he put it on the grate above the fire and stirred it round with a fork. In a few minutes, it was steaming.

Bundy got four tin plates, cups and spoons out of a wooden box under the shelf by the hearth and put them on the table. Just as he was about to attend to the beans again, Swift came in with the coffee water.

"Where's Teller? I told ya ta bring him in," Bundy said.

"I looked around but couldn't find him."

"Whatta ya mean ya couldn't find him? He was out there howlin' like a wolf a minute ago."

"Well, he ain't howlin' anymore. Maybe he went ta take a dump."

"Go find him, Ford," Bundy ordered.

"Hell, no, I ain't a-goin' out there. Teller kin go to hell fer all I care."

"Christ," Bundy growled, "I'll do it myself."

He walked quickly outside into the cold darkness. A full moon was just rising over the pines. He called out to Teller three times and waited for an answer. When he got no response he called out again, but much louder. As before, his calls were answered with a dead silence.

Suddenly a strange thing happened to Bundy. The hairs on the back of his neck tingled, and his neck grew warm. Someone or something was staring at him, and he could feel it. He tried to turn, but fear had control of his body and held it rigid. He whined like a baby as, from the corner of his left eye, he saw something move. A huge, black form came out of the woods, flying high in the air. It struck his left shoulder, knocking him off balance. He felt a sharp pain in his left arm as if slashed with a dull knife. Blood gushed down inside his coat sleeve. The thing landed on all fours a few feet away. Bundy saw two iridescent green eyes blazing up at him. As he reached for his gun it came at him again. This time it didn't miss.

Chapter 8

Toothless Mary wormed her way silently into the lives of Jim Settler and his daughter Laura. She did it in such a way that they never even noticed. The rancher was so absorbed in running the Rafter S Ranch he didn't realize what was happening. When he arose early in the morning, a pot of coffee was steaming on the stove and a plate of bacon, eggs and grits was already on the table. His and Laura's clothing were washed and hung on the clothesline on the west side of the house, and the wood box in the kitchen was kept full. The bed linen was cleaned and the blankets aired daily in the sun.

Even the rug in Settler's study came in for a good cleaning to remove all the mud tracks on it and the coffee stains spilled over it. The guns in the gun rack were dusted as was all the furniture. Fragrant scents floated about the living room from strategically placed sprigs of sweet sage. Brightly colored handmade clay pots filled with wild zinnia, yellow flax, charlock and marigold appeared on all the tables. And the amazing thing was, throughout all the time these activities were going on, Toothless Mary was practically invisible. Yet, she always appeared when needed.

At night, she slept at the foot of Laura's bed and watched over her in the daytime, attending to her every need. She had woven her invisible spider's web of dependence with great skill. Her victims, however, didn't yet realize it.

The day after Bundy, Teller, Swift and Ford had ridden out to hunt for wolves in the area around the west line shack, a good looking young man, dressed in a brown city suit, paid a call to the Settler's ranch. He arrived in a small carriage with a canvas top that was drawn by a single horse. It was similar to the kind seen in catalogues that were modeled after the English taxis in London that sheltered the passengers from the elements. But it differed from them in that it had no driver's box topside.

The young man climbed out of the carriage and tied the reins to the rail by the porch. He grabbed a doctor's bag from inside the boot well and walked up the porch steps. At this time, Settler was visiting Ty Nester at his farm. Seeing no one but Toothless Mary standing on the porch, the doctor walked up to greet her. "I'm Doctor Goodson," the young man said. "I'm here to see the patient."

The old Comanche woman waved Doctor Goodson in. Staying a few steps ahead of him, she led the young doctor into the hall and upstairs to Laura's bedroom. She smiled all the while, as if she had just heard a humorous joke. The door was open so Doctor Goodson marched right in. There was a scream, and the doctor jumped back out and stood cringing in the doorway with his back to the room. Toothless Mary suppressed a cackle.

"I beg your pardon, ma'am," the young doctor managed to say. "My sincere apologies."

"Go away, whoever you are!" Laura shouted out to him. "My father will thrash you good!"

"I'm Doctor Goodson," the doctor said defensively. "Doctor Tom Goodson?"

"What are you doing here? I'm not your patient."

"Your name was on Doctor Cutter's list. I'm his replacement."

There was a momentary pause before Laura replied, "Oh, well, alright. You can come in, then."

The young man turned slowly, and walked cautiously into Laura's bedroom. He saw that she had almost disappeared under the covers except for her nose, ears and eyes. He put his bag on the end table and took out a stethoscope. Once it was in place around his neck, he stood staring at Laura with a weak smile on his lips and his eyebrows raised. She avoided his stare as if it annoyed her.

"I'll have to touch you," he said. "To check your heart and lungs."

"Oh, alright, if you must."

"It would be better if you sat up."

Laura gave the doctor a glaring look. "Don't try anything."

"I won't."

The young girl wiggled herself into a sitting position. The doctor very cautiously sat on the edge of the bed.

"You'll have to lower the blanket."

"No, I don't think I'll do that."

"Alright, then I'll take your pulse if you'll permit me."

Laura thought about that for a moment then uncovered a small portion of her right arm, from the wrist to the fingers.

"Thank you, Mrs. Settler."

"Miss. I'm a Miss not a Mrs."

The doctor nodded and proceeded to take Laura's pulse. It was a bit strong, but from the blush on her cheeks he understood why. He smiled his most comforting smile at her.

"You seem to be doing well. May I look at where you were bitten by the wolf?"

"It's alright, it's fine. Mary has taken care of it."

"Has she put something on it?"

"Yes. She's an Indian healer."

The doctor looked over at Toothless Mary who was sitting in a chair by the door watching his every move. He smiled at her and said something. She nodded and said something back to him.

The doctor turned back to Laura. "She's Comanche. Her name is Tomasa. Her father was once a very important Comanche medicine man."

"Do you speak Comanche, Doctor?"

"A little. I apprenticed at a Comanche reservation in Utah for several years."

"What did you say to her?"

"I thanked her for taking such good care of you."

"What did she say to you?"

"She said white medicine men don't know much about anything and that she could teach me plenty."

Both Laura and the doctor laughed. The ice was broken. The doctor put his stethoscope away, and pulled a chair up close to the bed.

"I'm originally from Chicago," he said.

"Oh, really?"

"Yes."

"I attended a girl's school in Chicago," Laura told him.

"Oh?'

"Yes. Mrs. Tully's School for Girls."

"How did you like it?"

"She was mean. I hated it. I refused to go back and finish after my mother died. My father was furious, but I won him over. I can be very persuasive if I have to."

"I can imagine."

Toothless Mary left and came back with a tray with two cups of herbal tea, and some cookies made from flour and ground sunflower seeds. She gave it to Laura and the doctor and sat back in her chair to watch the doctor to make sure he properly behaved.

"She's adopted you," Doctor Goodson said. "She's taken you as her spirit daughter."

"She saved my life. I suppose she is my spiritual mother, in a way," Laura said.

"She'll always be loyal to you and try to protect you."

As Laura turned her head to look across the room at Toothless Mary, her hair parted exposing the strange markings on her forehead for a moment.

The doctor pointed and said, "I've seen those before, but never on a white person."

"Oh, really?"

"Yes, I think it's an ancient Comanche hex sign. I saw it once or twice on the reservation. None of the Indians would talk to me about it. Did she put them there?"

Knowing her story would sound crazy, Laura shrugged and replied, "I don't know. She could have. I was very sick for a while. I had a high fever and was very delirious."

"I'll ask her," the doctor replied.

He turned to look across the room at Toothless Mary, then spoke to her haltingly in Comanche. When he was finished she nodded and rattled away a long time, her voice rising and falling like waves on a beach. Her hands jerked and gyrated as they punctuated and emphasized her words. She got very emotional, and her eyes blazed like burning coals. At the end, she folded her arms, grunted and fell quiet.

"What did she say?" Laura asked. The doctor turned back to face her, saying nothing as he collected his thoughts.

Finally, he began his translation. "She said that once there were only the Comanche, the wolves and the buffalo. The wolves and the Comanche were brothers and hunted together. The wolves taught the Comanche braves how to shape-shift and become wolves like them so they could hunt together. They killed only as many buffalo as they needed to survive, and no more than that. The buffalo were everything to them. Without the buffalo, both the wolves and the Comanche could not survive in the winter."

The doctor stopped to collect his thoughts again, then went on.

"Then the white ghosts came and killed off all the buffalo and built their farms, ranches and towns on

Comanche land. They brought with them many cattle and sheep, took all the land for themselves and pushed the Comanche back into the hills and the high places. The Comanche became small in numbers while the white ghosts became large in numbers. Cattle soon walked where the buffalo once ran wild in numbers like the stars."

The young man paused again to arrange his words in the right order.

"Now the wolves and the shape-shifters are almost all gone. Those that remain have decided to fight on until the last of their breed have left this world and gone to the sacred hunting ground in the sky. But they have vowed they will kill as many white ghosts as they can. The only white ghosts safe from their wrath will be those with the mark of the wolf. According to her, a wolf did do it to save your life. She said it was a shape-shifter."

"A shape-shifter?" Laura said sarcastically. "Ridiculous! There's no such thing. It's probably an old Indian tale." She sat in silence, trying to absorb the meaning of Toothless Mary's story. "She has quite the imagination. My father thinks she's crazy, but harmless."

Tom Goodson shrugged. "Perhaps she's just a little strange. Indians don't think like we do. They live in a different world of their own."

Suddenly there was the sound of horses coming into the yard.

"It's my father," Laura said.

"I'd better go down to meet him," Goodson replied.

"Alright, but come back, won't you?"

The doctor nodded and smiled. "I'd be glad to come back, Miss Settler."

For the moment, the conversation about wolves was ended.

Chapter 9

It was late in the evening. Hunter and two of his cowboys rode into the yard of the Rafter S Ranch. From where he stood on the porch, Settler saw the bleak looks on their faces. Hunter kept Settler waiting until after he and his men had taken care of their horses. While the two cowboys went into the bunkhouse, Hunter walked over by the porch steps and looked up.

"This ain't good," Hunter said solemnly, shaking his head.

"What happened, Hunter?" Settler asked. "Did you go out there? Where are the hides?"

As he spoke, Hunter slowly began rolling a cigarette. "Oh, we went out there alright, but there weren't any hides. As a matter of fact, there wasn't anything there that you'd wanna see."

"What the hell do you mean there wasn't anything there that I'd wanna see?" Settler sounded skeptical. He chuckled nervously. "What are you talking about? You told me Bundy and his boys would kill some wolves. Well, did they, or didn't they?"

Hunter nodded. "Oh, there was some killin' done out there, alright," he said. He finished rolling his cigarette and lit it. When the match flared up Settler saw the stark look in the ramrod's eyes. "But it wasn't Bundy and his men what done the killin'. No sir, not by a long shot."

"What the hell are you talking about, Hunter?" Settler growled in frustration. "Spit it out!"

"Sure, I'll spit it out, but you ain't gonna like it. We saw parts of bodies layin' all around on the ground in front of the shack. They were so chewed up and torn to bits we couldn't tell who was who, except for the clothes clinging to their bones. Some were missing legs, and some were missing arms. Others had their heads chewed clean off. They must have been alive when it happened because their eyeballs popped out."

The rancher stood stone-faced staring out into the field as if searching for something to hold onto, to help him keep his sanity. He finally shook his head, looking dazed and confused. He didn't know how to respond. "That's crazy!" he finally said, laughing nervously.

"It might be crazy," the big ramrod said. "But it's the truth. The boys will back up every word I jest said."

"Good God! I can't believe it. What's going on, Hunter? What's happening out there?"

"I don't know. I just don't know," Hunter said in a weary voice. He looked defeated, overwhelmed. "We got all their belts and guns," Hunter said. "They're in the saddlebags."

"What about their mounts and the pack horse?"

"It looks like they broke lose. One left its reins still tied to the rail. They must have been spooked pretty bad," Hunter replied. "I figure some of the blood on the ground might have been from the horses as they fought ta get away from the wolves."

"My God! This is unbelievable!"

"We had to hold our noses from the smell of blood and urine. Seems as all the wolves in the world took a good pee on the line shack. The smell woulda knocked over an elephant."

That last remark made Settler break out into a sad, sarcastic laugh. He shook his head and rubbed his neck in dismay. Nothing he had ever experienced in his entire life had come close to this. The cattle lost to wolves were tolerable, except in the west sector. It was there that, for some unexplainable reason, the wolves seemed to have chosen to assemble in large numbers. It was also closest to the ranch house, the center of activity. One would think they would have picked the more remote north or east sectors to hunt. But no, they were blatantly operating right under Settler's nose. And they boldly flaunted it in his face by urinating en masse on the line shack. That was the last straw!

"Alright," Settler finally said. "Get the boys and go eat. Parker has a hot meal waiting for all of you. After that, get some rest."

Hunter left Settler standing alone on the porch. It was getting noticeably colder. The rancher looked up at the low, grey clouds and turned his coat collar higher. He shook his head in frustration, wondering what he could or should do. Perhaps it was wiser to let it alone and hope the problem would solve itself, as problems sometimes do. But with winter coming on, that wasn't likely. In fact, more wolves might come into the area. There was plenty of empty land behind the west sector where they could hide. It would take an army of men to flush them out, and Settler didn't have the men or the time for that. He had a ranch to run.

The rancher walked back to his house, into the warmth of the kitchen. A fire blazed, and a pot of coffee was waiting on the big stove. The soup pot, filled with beef, carrots and turnips, was steaming next to it. A plate piled high with sourdough biscuits and a small bowl with salted bacon fat sat on the kitchen table. A wild berry pie sat near the biscuits. At the far end of the table a basket woven from broom sedge held dried milkweed pods, a sprig of pine and a sprig of mistletoe. A place was set for one.

Settler poured a cup of coffee, filled a bowl with stew and sat down to eat. Occasionally, he looked around to see if he could spot the old Indian woman. He felt her presence. She was unseen, yet always there. She seemed to sense his needs. He wondered why she bothered to please him. When he was finished, he went upstairs to see Laura. She was sitting in bed reading a book.

"Have you eaten yet, honey?"

"Oh, sure, an hour ago, Dad."

The rancher pulled a chair up near the bed. "What are you reading?"

"A book by an English writer named Charles Dickens. Doctor Goodson gave it to me."

"You two are getting on pretty good, aren't you?"

"It seems that way, Dad."

Settler wasn't at all impressed with the young doctor. He was a city boy, not a rancher. He preferred that Laura marry Tobey Nester or a rancher's son. That's where all the money was, not in a doctor treating people who, half the time, were too poor to pay.

"I'm getting out of bed tomorrow, Dad," Laura said. "It'll be good to be about again."

"But you won't be riding yet, will you?"

"Maybe in a week. We'll see what the doctor says."

Settler nodded. "Of course. See what Doctor Goodson says." Laura detected a bit of sarcasm in her father's tone.

They chatted a while. Settler was careful not to mention what happened out at the west line shack. He decided to wait for a better time, when Laura was fully recovered.

Finally, he went downstairs to his study to relax, but, like iron to a magnet, his mind turned to the wolves. He took a slow mental inventory of possible ways to get rid of them. The status quo was no longer tolerable. It was a matter of pride as well as necessity. Besides that, his reputation was at stake. Now he was expected to avenge the death of his men, and he had no idea how he could go about doing that.

The rancher didn't know it then but the solution to his wolf problem was coming his way, and it would turn out to be his worst nightmare.

Chapter 10

It was a dull, grey afternoon in November. Feathers of snow began falling. Settler and Laura were in the kitchen when they heard rattling and clanging outside. It kept getting louder. Struck with curiosity, they hurried out to the porch. Hunter and two Rafter S men, Travis and Foley, heard it, too. They stopped working on the corral gate, walked across the yard and stood leaning on the fence.

After about five minutes of waiting, they saw a ghostly prairie schooner, drawn by two oxen, materialize out of the dense, foggy haze that forms when cold air and warm air meet close to the ground. The oxen ambled along the road at a leisurely pace. They finally turned into the snow-covered field on the other side of the road, across from the yard, puffing vapor clouds from their nostrils. The wagon stopped there and the oxen buried their faces in the snow, foraging for dried field grass.

It looked like any other prairie schooner, except that it had large, black, commercially painted letters on its white canvas sides. The lettering read: *Uriah Gault - Predator Control*. Below that was the promise: *Results Guaranteed*.

The schooner was driven by a man who wore a black leather hat. The brim of the hat was so wide it covered everything except his protruding, whiskered chin. His short, wide torso was covered by a high collared bearskin greatcoat and his legs were encased in knee high drover's boots. The man's gloveless hands were large, and gnarled like roots of a tree. His arms were excessively long for his body. Thusly, covered in fur, the man had a simian appearance about him. It looked as if the wagon were being driven by a gorilla or an ape.

Laura turned to her father and remarked, "Who is that, Dad?"

"I have no idea," Settler said. He walked down the porch steps, through the flurries and up to the yard gate near Hunter, Travis and Foley. Once there, the rancher yelled, "Howdy, stranger!"

The man turned his head in Settler's direction, shifted the reins from his right hand to his left hand and saluted Settler by touching the brim of his hat. "Is your name, by any chance, James Settler?" he asked in a deep, gruff, gravelly voice.

Settler had already classified this person as a traveling salesman. He'd want to sell the lady of the house the newest versions of pots, pans and can openers. He probably sold tools, too, and would offer to sharpen knives, scissors and axes. But, by the looks of the lettering on the canvas sides, this one also specialized in selling poison powders for killing rats, raccoons, squirrels, and other pests that invaded prairie households. And, of course, he hoped to end up being invited to dinner after being on the road for such a long time.

"That's right, I'm Jim Settler. What can I do for you mister?"

"The question is, what can I do for you, sir," the man replied in a booming voice that rang above the whining of the November wind. His voice did, however, reveal a certain level of education and experience above that of your average snake-oil salesman. His tone and timbre reminded Settler of a preacher he once knew.

The rancher glanced over at the two oxen and then back at the man. "Alright, mister, what can you do for me?" There was a hint of impatience in Settler's voice.

"Thank you for asking, sir," the man replied. He crawled down from the wagon, stretched out his overly long arms, then ambled along on short legs to the yard gate where Settler and the others stood. He acknowledged Hunter, Travis and Foley with a salute. Upon seeing Laura on the porch, he waved and shouted, "Good day to you, Miss Laura. I trust you are feeling better, ma'am?"

Caught by surprise, Laura merely nodded, wondering how he knew her name and condition.

"We're not buying anything," Settler said flatly. He resented the man's attitude of familiarity with his daughter.

By way of deflecting the rancher's remark, the man said, "I was passing through town, sir, when I met Doctor Goodson?" He ended the sentence as a question, rather than a statement of fact.

"Yes, I know him. Did he send you all this way just to see me?"

"As a matter of fact, he did suggest you might be interested in my products."

"And what might they be, sir?"

"Perhaps you'd like to see for yourself, Mr. Settler."

The rancher hesitated then sighed as if annoyed. "Alright," he said after a moment's hesitation, "but I don't want to delay you. You probably have someplace to go."

"Actually, sir, not at all."

The man scampered to the back of the wagon. Settler shrugged, looked at the others, then followed behind. This strange looking man unlatched the chain, opened the rear gate and stood anxiously by, waiting for Settler and the cowboys. Once they got in position, he went into what sounded like a memorized speech.

"Behold, sir, the answer to all your problems. These instruments and potions are guaranteed to rid you of the predatory *Canis lupus*! Why, just a month ago, up in Colby County, by my methods, I successfully pacified several packs of predators within two weeks' time. I have endorsements from ranchers all through this great state, testimonials that verify the veracity of my claims."

The man paused to catch his breath before delivering the rest of his pitch. Settler noticed his voice had a distinct nasal quality to it.

"The *Canis lupus* is a cunning predator, sir. He is one of the Devil's most malicious creations. Although he only has a life span averaging about twelve years and weighs but 180 pounds, he has managed to propagate and multiply throughout the forests and plains of the entire earth, despite being the most hunted animal in the world. On the surface, in comparison to other animals, he has no extra powers, but what powers he does have he uses wisely. He can smell blood from two miles away and humans rarely get closer than a thousand yards of him."

This strange man paused again to see the effects of his words on his audience. Satisfied that he had their attention, he went on.

"Although his top running speed is about 37 miles per hour, and a deer can run faster at 47 miles an hour, he surrounds his prey with as many as twenty of his fellow creatures, enclosing it in a trap from which there is no escape. He can outrun your average horse and easily outrun a cow. Since a cow can only manage to run, at best, 20 miles per hour, you can see why he prefers them over other forms of prey. Not only are cows slower, they also have much more meat to offer than a deer or horse. And the meat is more succulent and tender and less dry and stringy than deer meat."

He stopped his pitch there, crawled up into the back of the wagon and opened a wooden crate. He reached in and pulled out a large saw toothed, spring-operated animal trap. Scampering to the opening again, he leaned over and handed it down to Settler.

"Take a look at this, my friend."

The rancher took the heavy metal object in his hands, turning it around and over. Finally, he nodded and handed it over to Hunter for inspection. He examined it, then gave it to Travis and Foley. They all seemed impressed. Settler handed it back to the man.

"Made in Chicago from the finest spring steel, my friends," the man said emphatically. Then, "But that's not all."

With the trap in hand, he crawled a second time towards the back of the wagon and got a pair of rubber gloves. He put them on, went to a box with a lid, opened it and took out a glass jar with a screw top. Crawling forward again, he held the jar up to the light for all to see. It was full of small pellets seemingly made by hand from some variety of vegetation.

"This my friends, is genus *Aconitum*, also known as monkshood, devil's helmet or wolf's bane. It is one of the deadliest natural poisons known to mankind. It kills within hours. There's burning and tingling of the mouth, vomiting and diarrhea and fire in the stomach. Numbness spreads to the limbs and heart, and organ failure soon follows. Just one touch of these little darlings on the bare flesh is a sentence of death."

The man hustled rearward, replaced the jar in the box, removed the gloves, then came forward and climbed back down onto the ground.

"My name is Uriah Gault, Mr. Settler," he said. "If you are interested, my specialty is, as my sign says, controlling predators."

Settler assumed the whole town knew about his losing battle with the wolves. Most likely, the entire valley knew. And now this man, Uriah Gault, also knew. Only, he had come to offer his services. But the price was yet to be determined. He stared at the man. His face was mostly hidden by his hat. Settler wondered if it looked as ape-like as his body. When Jim Settler did business with a man, he liked to look him in the eyes. The easiest way to get him to remove his hat was to invite him in for dinner.

"Mr. Gault," Settler said, "if you'd care to, we could go in where it's warm and talk. It's about dinner time, and we have a pot of turnip and beef stew on the stove."

"That's very good of you, sir," Uriah Gault said. "I'm much obliged."

Gault tied up the tailgate and walked alongside Settler into the yard. It almost seemed as if the rancher were walking alongside a large ape. Hunter, Travis and Foley noticed this and chuckled as they went down to the mess tent to eat.

Settler took his guest up on the porch and introduced him to Laura. Settler could see the look of revulsion on his daughter's face upon seeing this odd-looking man up close.

Gault stared at her for a moment. He showed no sign that he noticed the markings through the hair covering her forehead.

Once in the kitchen, Gault removed his hat and Settler saw his face in the shadow of a flickering oil lamp. He did, indeed, have facial features matching his simian body. His bullet shaped head was small and oblong with a wide, protruding chin. His forehead and nose were flat, and two small, beady black eyes peered out from recessed sockets. Short, thick, dark hair covered the sides of his face. Longer hair formed a widow's peak on his forehead. It covered his head and hung down over his sloping, narrow shoulders. Settler and his daughter found it difficult not to stare.

Over dinner Gault didn't ask any questions about the marks on her forehead. Laura assumed that either he was being polite and discrete, or else his eyesight was too poor to see through her hair.

"This is wonderful stew," Mr. Gault said. "Delicious."

"Toothless Mary made it," Laura replied.

"Yes, Doctor Goodson mentioned her. Is she around? I don't see her."

"She likes to keep to herself," Laura replied. "Actually, she doesn't like white people very much."

"I can understand that, given the history of the two races."

"Yes," Laura agreed, "given the history of the two races."

"But we finally put them in their place," Gault said boastfully.

Neither Settler or his daughter replied to that. Laura was of the conviction that the old Comanche woman would not like this killer of wolves very much. To her it was the same as killing a Comanche warrior. Later in Settler's den, the two men talked about the price.

"How much do you charge, Mr. Gault?"

"Two dollars a wolf is my going price."

"That seems reasonable, sir."

"Do you have any use for the pelts?" Gault asked

"No, I don't."

"Then you won't mind if I keep them. I can sell them in town."

"You can have them, then," Settler replied.

It was dark and much colder when Gault walked back to his wagon. He unhitched the two oxen, tied them to a scrub oak on a long line, and climbed into the back of the wagon where he had a small makeshift kitchen and bed. He secured a piece of canvas over the open end, then lit an oil lamp to warm the place up. The wind howled and rocked the wagon. Gault sat on the edge of his makeshift cot and stared blankly at the flapping canvas. He finally lay back, but not to sleep. He never slept. In sleep, the nightmares came, and he dreaded them more than anything else. So, he hardly every slept.

Chapter 11

In a gathering in the bunkhouse, Gault introduced himself to the cowboys and explained how he planned to deal with the wolves. They stared at the odd looking little man, fascinated by his physical appearance. Never in all their days had they seen anything like Uriah Gault. They'd be telling jokes and tales about him for a long time after he was gone. But now they held their chuckles, and listened attentively as he revealed his plan. When he was finished, he got several bottles of whiskey from his wagon and they sat around drinking and talking. The subject was mostly about wolves. Gault mesmerized them with his strange stories. By evening they saw him in a different light and liked him much better.

The following day was brisk and cold. With the cowboys on their horses and Gault in a buckboard, they started out for the west sector with a dozen traps and a bottle of pellets. On the way, they stopped, shot a calf and tossed its body into the buckboard with the traps. By mid-afternoon they arrived at the west line shack.

Gault put on gloves and a dirty apron, took a knife from the side pocket on his right boot, and then cut a dozen small chunks of meat from the calf's body. Taking a stick, he poked a hole into each steak and stuffed pellets into the holes. With that done, he tied a long string around one end of each piece of meat. Next, he cut twelve more poisoned steaks for the traps and loaded the meat into the buckboard. Finally, he had Hunter, Travis and Foley move the buckboard behind the line shack.

"String them up, boys," he said, "but try not to touch the meat or you'll leave your scent on it."

While Travis and Foley hung the poisoned meat on low hanging tree branches, Hunter set the traps in the woods. Still wearing his gloves, Gault went behind him and carefully tied a piece of poisoned meat on the trip-lever of each trap then cocked it. Each trap had a short, iron chain with a long spike. Gault had one of the cowboys hammer the spikes into the half-frozen ground. Finally, Gault got a cake of lye soap from a small box he had brought along, and they all went down to the nearby stream and washed their hands. Gault also washed the gloves.

Now that the work was done, they retreated to the line shack to get warm and eat a hasty meal of jerky and hardtack. After that, they started back to the ranch. It turned much colder, and a harsh wind pushed at their backs all the way to the ranch. Darkness was near when they rode in. Settler met them in front of the corral. Snow flurries began to swirl about them.

"How did it go, boys?" Settler asked, blowing on his hands to warm them. His breath came out in little puffs of white vapor.

"Pretty good," Hunter said. "There wasn't much to it."

The rancher looked at Gault. "What's next?"

Gault replied, "We go back out there tomorrow and count the kills."

"How many do you expect to get?" Settler asked.

"Twelve will die in the traps. Another twelve will die from the hanging meat. They'll try to help the ones caught in the traps even though they've eaten the poisoned meat hanging from the branches. One or two might get lucky and get away, but I doubt it." Gault spoke casually, without emotion.

"Jesus!" Settler heard himself saying solemnly.

Hunter, Travis and Lewis stared at the rancher, wondering why their boss sounded so sad. He was supposed to be pleased that his problem with the wolves was finally coming to an end. And at only two dollars a head. What could be better than that? After all these years, he would emerge the victor. How many wolves could there be? Twenty, thirty, forty? Even if there were a hundred or two hundred, at two dozen a day, it wouldn't take more than two weeks to kill every one of them.

"It'll be over real soon," Hunter said to Settler. "Mr. Gault knows what he's doing."

Settler smiled weakly and nodded. "Good," he replied, adding, "Let's hope this works."

"You have my guarantee, Mr. Settler," Gault replied, "my personal guarantee."

Settler turned to his men. "You boys must be starved. Finish taking care of the horses and then see Marty Parker. He has some hot food waiting for you." Turning to Uriah Gault he said, "Would you like to come up to the house for a bite?"

"Thank you, sir, I would like that very much."

Hunter, Travis and Foley walked their mounts and the buckboard horse down towards the barn while Gault and Settler went quickly up to the ranch house. They went into the kitchen where Toothless Mary and Laura were putting the finishing touches to the evening meal of steak, mashed turnips, pole beans and gravy. A wild strawberry tart rested on the stove top over to one side, keeping warm. For a moment, the trapper and the Indian woman stared at each other, then Toothless Mary quickly left.

"Is that her?" Gault asked. His eyes followed her out of the room.

"Yes," the rancher said.

"She's skitterish, isn't she?"

"A little," Settler replied.

Laura poured coffee. The three of them sat down at the kitchen table. No one spoke as they ate. They could hear the wind howling outside. The windows rattled and shook in the walls.

"Tell me, Mr. Gault," Laura asked near the end of the meal, "How did you get into the business of trapping wolves?"

Gault hesitated a moment before answering. "It's a long story, Miss Settler," the trapper said in his deep, hollow voice, looking up from his plate as he spoke, "but if you wish, I'll gladly tell it to you."

"Please do, sir," Laura replied without hesitating. She studied his simian face and felt sorry for him. Nature had done him a disservice, leaving him with animal like features, a face frozen in an angry grimace even when he wasn't angry.

"As you wish," Gault said, trying to smile but only managing a grotesque grin that looked like he was smiling and crying at the same time. He sipped his coffee, settled back in his chair and began.

"My parents were members of a small, traveling group of performers in what is commonly referred to as a carnival freak show. It roamed throughout the territories. My mother suffered from a physical abnormality knows as dwarfism, and was referred to as a midget. She wore black makeup and was billed as a savage pygmy cannibal. My father suffered from an affliction medically called hypertrichosis, or the werewolf disease. It is a disease where the entire human body is covered with an excess of hair."

Gault stopped a moment to study the faces of father and daughter, to see the effects of his words. Settler nodded and Laura said calmly, and with understanding, "I see. Go on."

"I was a little boy when..." Gault cut the sentence off and started again. "I was a young boy of five when the carnival headed for Denver, Colorado. We had been weeks on the trail, on our way from California across the territories of Nevada and Utah. We were high in the mountains, about fifty miles from Denver, when our wagons got bogged down in a terrible snow storm. It was early February, the coldest time of the year out there. The snow got too deep to go on."

The trapper stopped to roll a cigarette with his huge, gnarled hands. Laura watched as they quickly, and neatly did the job. Gault took the oil lamp off the table and used it to light the cigarette. After inhaling and blowing out a huge cloud of grey smoke at the ceiling, he settled down again.

"That's when the wolves came to get us. We had no guns or rifles, nothing but a few axes, hammers and shovels, is all. We had food for only a few days. The wolves must have smelled our helplessness They came each night and dragged some of us off, four or five at a time. None of us knew how to fight them. They were quiet, quick, and very strong. We were too slow, too frightened. There were a lot of them. Sometimes they fought each other over the bodies. By the sixth day, there were seven of us left. That's when my mother took my clothes off and covered my body with axle grease. She plastered it thickly all over my little, hairy body, using it all up on me. In the cold air, it formed a firm cover. After she was finished, she placed me in the back of a wagon."

Gault stopped, drew in heavily on the cigarette and sent out a plume of smoke. It swirled above the kitchen table and finally faded into nothingness. He went on again.

"I heard them screaming as the wolves came to get my father and mother and the few others left. After that, the wolves looked around for more to eat. Several of them jumped into the back of the wagon and sniffed at me. I lay still and pretended to be made of wood. The smell of the axle grease wasn't to their liking so they went away. After they were gone I lay in the back of the wagon for three days until I was found by some Cheyenne Indians. They cleaned me up, put clothes on me and took me to Fort Logan in Denver. An old couple there took me in. The children in school made fun of me. I had to fight each day to survive because I looked different. But I never blamed them. They did what children naturally do, treat others cruelly who are different from them.

Gault stopped again when Laura lifted a hand to indicate she had a question.

"I'm so sorry for losing your parents, Mr. Gault," Laura said, "especially under such awful circumstances. It leads me to assume that you must hate wolves very much, do you not, sir?"

"You are correct in that assumption, Miss Settler," Gault replied. "In fact, for years after the incident, I wondered how I could best find a way to get revenge on them for the death of my parents."

"I see you finally found one."

"Yes. I saw trappers bringing in animal skins at Fort Logan. I read books and magazines on trapping, and found work with an old trapper there. I trapped with him for five years. It was he who put me on to wolf's bane. It grew wild in the mountain valleys." Gault smiled his strange smile. "Now that you know my story, Miss Settler, perhaps you would tell me yours?" He pointed at the marks on Laura's forehead.

Laura sipped her coffee while she thought what to say. She really had no answer to the question that would make any sense to anyone. Her father had asked her that same question and all she could say was that she didn't know how the marks got there. The easiest thing to do was to lie.

"The old woman put it there," Laura replied, smiling. "She said it's to protect me from shape-shifters, whatever they are."

"They're probably ghosts," Gault said, laughing. "Indians see ghosts in every nook and cranny and under every rock."

After they had a piece of the wild strawberry tart, Gault thanked his hosts and retreated to his wagon. He lit his oil lamp and sat on his cot, heaving a deep sigh. It had been a busy day. But he had to admit the rancher and his daughter had been very civil after they had gotten over the shock of his appearance. He had to give them that. Yes, they were good people. He would help them with their problem and then move on, as he always did. No one seemed to want him around permanently. And why should they? He was not exactly the type of person anyone would like to introduce to friends or invite to a party. Small children and even older ones stared at him in horror and disgust. Uriah Gault's trail was a lonesome trail to travel.

Outside, the wind howled but Gault's ears heard another howling above that. It was the howling of the wolves. Many, many wolves. Gault smiled inwardly. Soon there would be less of them howling. He was ready to do battle.

Chapter 12

There was a wolf in her room. It was a huge wolf with coal black fur and large, glowing green eyes. It climbed up on the bed and stood over her. Staring down into her eyes for a moment, it then lifted its right front leg and pressed its paw against her forehead. She felt the points of its nails burn into her flesh like a red-hot iron. Then she would awaken and let out a sigh of relief, knowing it was only that dream again. It came often.

Her father had asked her what had happened that day when she rode out and was attacked by the wolves. All she told him was, after she was bitten, she fainted and couldn't remember anything after that. But that was a lie. She did not lose consciousness and was aware of what was happening to her, although most of it was dim and confusing. It was as if someone had dropped a translucent shroud over her head.

After something or someone had frightened away the wolf that had bitten her, she felt herself being lifted and carried down into a shadowy glen. There was a cave in a rock wall there, and whoever held her put her gently down on a bed of soft pine boughs. She could hear water running nearby and caught the sweet scent of wild lilacs.

By then, she had a fever and was burning up. She asked for water and it was given to her in a gourd. The thing that gave it to her was shaped like a man, but she couldn't see clearly because she was delirious. It rolled up her shirt sleeve to expose the wound just above her right elbow. Suddenly the shadowy figure seemed to oscillate and shimmer. It changed shape right before her eyes and became a big, black wolf with blazing green eyes. She started to scream as it bent over her, but when it began licking her wound, she stopped. Its tongue was warm and soothing and her wound was soon clean and dry.

When the beast was finished, it stood staring down at her. She lay in a half-dream state, with her eyes closed and her mind in a fog of delirium. A voice forced its way into in her head. It sounded like the voice of an old person. She looked up to see an old grey wolf standing alongside the huge black one. It glanced down at her, then turned to the big black one.

"*Shu-dah-gay-lah*, the white ghost cannot stay here. She is not part of us," a calm, ancient voice said inside her mind. It came from the old grey wolf.

"But, she is part of me, *Mat-tu-say-lah*," the big black wolf replied. Laura could hear his voice, too.

"How can that be, *Shu-dah-gay-lah?*" the old grey wolf asked.

"I knew her mother," the big black wolf replied. "I saw her beauty and I shape-shifted. She and I became as one."

"Then the blood of the wolf is mixed with this white ghost's blood."

"Yes. When I saw her face, I knew she was my daughter."

"But she must go. Your brothers and sisters are getting angry. She was the prey of *Ah-say-nu-lah*, and you took her away from him. He is very angry and so are the others," the old voice said.

"I will fight them for her. She is *Nee-lah-sol-lah*, my daughter."

"She is only a part of you, *Shu-dah-gay-lah*, the part that can shape-shift. The other part of you is wolf. It cannot stand and walk with her. There will always be that between you."

"Then what am I to do, Grandfather? Can you tell me?"

"Take her back to her people. I will tell the others to leave her alone."

"Is there no other path?"

"No, there is only that one path."

"Alright. I will let her rest a while and, when the moon is high, I will take her home."

"So be it. I will tell the others to let you pass freely."

The black wolf lay down by Laura's side, its body close to hers. She could feel the heat of the fur. It kept her warm. After a while she stopped shivering and put a hand on its neck. It pressed its head against her shoulder.

During the next few hours, Laura Settler lay in a delirious sleep. The old grey wolf came into the den and pressed its paw against her forehead. It burned. She awoke complaining and the old grey wolf left. She slept again, this time peacefully. A few hours later the black wolf stood up and nudged her. She struggled to her feet, leaned over and lay flat on its back with her arms about its neck and her head alongside its head. The creature moved slowly out into the night until it came to the wide field of sedge. As it loped to the southeast through the dark of night, she could feel its powerful muscles rippling under the soft, warm fur. She heard a voice in her head say, "I will take you home, *Nee-lah-sol-lah*. I will watch over you and keep you safe."

"Why did the grey one hurt me?" she heard her mind-voice ask.

The black wolf's mind-voice replied, "It was to save you, my daughter."

"From what? From who?"

"From the wolves."

After that, there were no more voices in her head, only the howling of wolves far behind them.

Chapter 13

Jim Settler had concluded that Tom Goodson was interested in his daughter Laura for other reasons than just being her doctor. Now that she was up and about, he came to see her frequently. Once they went on a picnic to a covert glade by a clear stream a few miles from the ranch house. She had him come to dinner often and he brought her books and flowers. He took an interest in her general physical condition and monitored her wound, which was healing nicely. Because he refused money for his services, Settler knew Goodson had a personal reason for the visits. He didn't know if Laura was aware of it, but the rancher figured he'd mention it to her, to get her opinion on the subject.

"Doctor Goodson comes around a lot lately, doesn't he, honey?"

"Yes, Dad. What about it?"

"Has he said anything to you?"

"About what?"

"About him maybe being interested in you more than just as a patient or a friend?"

"Not yet, Dad."

"Do you think he will?"

They were sitting in the kitchen over dinner. Toothless Mary had cooked them roast chicken with carrots and potatoes from the root cellar. As usual, she had gone off somewhere in the house to be by herself. Settler's mind was on the trapper, Gault. The rancher was anxious to hear how many wolves would be killed, how high the death count would be.

Settler forced his attention back to his daughter and said, "I think Tobey Nester is still waiting for your answer. Have you talked to him?"

"No, and there's no need to, Dad. I'm not interested in him. Besides, I hear he's courting Nancy Miller from the Bar M spread."

Settler shrugged. He didn't want to get in another argument like the last one when Laura rode out and was attacked by wolves, so he backed off.

"I see," was all he said.

When they had finished eating, Settler got up, put on his hat and mackinaw and walked out onto the porch to roll a cigarette. There were only one or two cowboys in the bunkhouse. Hunter had sent most of them out to the north and east sectors, but he had gone to the west sector with Gault, Travis and Foley to check on the traps.

The rancher sat in a rocking chair and thought about the wolves. He had heard stories and rumors about how they chose certain parcels of land as their territory. They formed into groups of ten or twenty and defended an area as large as fifty square miles or more, marking their boundaries with urine and feces. Once they settled in, they fought to defend their homes. There was a human aspect to that. Didn't human settlers do the same, fight to defend their families and their homes? Just as the Indians also did?

For a moment Settler felt a tightening in his stomach, a feeling of uncertainty, a questioning of his relationship with the balance of nature. The wolves had been in the west sector for as long as he could remember and had been culling cattle at a steady rate for years. The rustlers were doing the very same thing, so why was it especially wrong when wolves did it? Wolves only killed what they needed to survive, while rustlers stole hundreds, even thousands of cattle, and sold them for financial gain. So, why kill the wolves and let the rustlers go?

Didn't he, Jim Settler, as a man, not have a God given mandate to live in peace and harmony with the natural world around him? Some people thought that man, because he was the dominant species, could ignore that obligation. Those humans who lived close to nature and depended on it for survival had developed other doctrines. The Indians, closest of all to the earth, had their own tenets and creeds.

The Navajos called it *hozho*. It meant living in balance and harmony with nature. The Lakota called it *wawoohola*, having compassion and respect for all of the creator's creatures. The Ojibwa called it *ninoododadiwin*, existing in harmony with the earth and all living things. Throughout the savage West, people of the earth had developed high ideals to help them coexist with nature.

That was one side of the scale. On the other was the death of Settler's men, Bundy, Swift, Ford and Teller. He couldn't pretend it didn't happen, and he couldn't just forget it or ignore it. Nor could he leave it unanswered. As a rancher, it was his obligation to avenge the killing of his men. It was the code, and now it conflicted with nature.

Settler's thoughts were suddenly interrupted by the sound of horses out on the road. Moments later Hunter, Travis and Foley rode through the gate and into the yard laughing and smiling. Gault came behind in the buckboard. It was piled high with wolf skins. They stopped a few feet from the porch steps. Settler stood up from the rocking chair and walked down to meet them. The smell of recently skinned wolves was sickening.

"How many?" the rancher asked. There was no enthusiasm in his words. The lust for revenge had gone out of him, and he couldn't understand why. He would sort it out later, when he was alone.

"Twenty," Hunter said as he dismounted. "The hanging meat got twelve, and the traps got eight."

"Then four got away?" Settler asked.

Foley chuckled. "They got away, alright, but they left part of their legs in the traps."

"How did that happen?" the rancher asked.

"Easy, they chewed their own damn legs off at the lower joint," Travis laughed with a big grin. "Now we got some three-legged wolves a-runnin' around out there."

Gault was studying Settler's face to see his reaction. The rancher felt it and turned to him. "How did it go, Mr. Gault?"

"Very smooth, Mr. Settler, very smooth. Your men were very helpful. It went very well."

Hunter looked at Settler and said, "We'll put the pelts in the drying shed, then we'll see Parker about some grub."

Settler nodded. "Alright. Have your men take care of the buckboard horse so Mr. Gault can wash up." He addressed Gault. "Come to the house for dinner when you're finished washing, Mr. Gault."

The trapper was quick to respond. "If it's all the same to you, Settler, I'll just go ahead and eat with the boys."

For a moment Settler was taken aback, but he quickly covered it up. "Yes, of course, Mr. Gault, whatever you want."

As Settler walked back up towards the ranch house, he suddenly felt that something was going on behind his back. He sensed that Gault and Hunter were up to something. He'd have to find out what it was.

Chapter 14

Settler and his daughter were in the kitchen at the table finishing breakfast and soaking up the warmth of the old cast iron stove when Gault, Hunter, Travis and Foley left for the west sector. The wind roared around the ranch house, rattling the windows and doors.

Laura started the conversation. "Dad, is the wolf situation really all that bad?"

"What do you mean by 'all that bad'?"

"Well, I'm just trying to figure out just how bad the wolf situation is in the west sector, Dad."

"It's bad enough. We're losing maybe 21 cows a week. That adds up to about 84 cows a month. Putting that on a yearly basis, that's about 1,000 cows a year."

"That sure sounds like a lot of cows."

"Yes, it is," Settler replied seriously.

Laura gave it some thought, then replied, "So, you're saying we're losing about three cows a day. Is that right."

"That's about right."

"Three cows a day means there are about 200 wolves roaming the west sector."

"How did you figure that out?"

"A grown wolf, on average, eats twelve pounds of meat a day. A cow carries about 800 pounds of fat and meat."

"What does that have to do with anything?"

"One cow would feed about 65 wolves a day. So, three cows a day means there are maybe 200 wolves in the west sector, more or less."

"If you put it that way, I guess so."

"What about the other sectors, north and east?"

"Well, we lose maybe two or three cows a week, at most. I'm not really worried about them."

Laura got a pencil and piece of paper from the cupboard drawer and sat back down at the kitchen table.

"How many cows do we have, all told, Dad?"

"About thirty thousand." The rancher scratched his head. "You sure are asking a lot of questions this morning, girl. How come?"

Laura ignored the question and asked, "How many bulls do we have?"

"Right now? About three hundred."

"How many cows will a bull sire a year?"

"On average, about 40 cows a year." Settler chuckled again. The questions seemed silly to him.

Laura wrote down some figures on the paper, then looked up and said, "Three hundred bulls and 30,000 cows can produce 12,000 calves a year, right?"

"Well, there are some losses. You can shave off a few hundred, just to be real about it."

"Alright, let's be really conservative and say 11,000 calves a year, then."

"Okay, what's your point?"

"My point is that if the herd increases by 11,000 calves a year, and we lose 1,000 cows a year to the west sector wolves, there's still a net gain of 10,000 calves. Isn't that right?"

"Yeah, I'd say that's about right," Settler replied as he nodded and smiled. "You know, I never sat down to figure it out that way. I was always so riled up all I could think of were those dead cows. It just seemed awful to me. And Hunter was always at me about fighting back and wiping them out. I guess it ain't as bad as it seems after all. As long as the killings don't increase, I guess we can tolerate the loss."

"How long has the kill rate been three a day in the west sector?"

"For about two years now."

"Then the wolf population has stabilized. I think it will stay that way there."

"What about the other two sectors, north and east, Laura?" Settler asked.

"We'll keep an eye on them, Dad. Even if they increase, the herd will still increase faster, thanks to the bulls, and we'll have more bulls next year, won't we?"

"I expect so."

Settler looked at his daughter with renewed respect. She had shown him the way to stop killing the wolves, something that had gone against his grain since Gault had started his operation. Especially now that he knew the man's motive was personal. Gault wasn't a professional trapper, he was an exterminator. His goal in life was to wipe out an entire species.

The fact was, when the big herd was discovered down in the Nueces, in Texas, years ago, there were millions of cattle and thousands of wolves and other predators existing side by side. Still, the great herd grew by the thousands. There was a balance of nature at work. Man had upset that balance, depriving the natural predators such as wolves of the food nature had provided for them.

In a way, it was very sad. In Gault's own mind he was justified because of the killing of his parents by the wolves. But now, Settler felt he had to put a stop to it. In a sense, these were his wolves. They depended upon him, now that the buffalo were gone. He had to secure their survival.

"What do you want me to do?"

"Pay Gault off and send him away, Dad. Let him do his killing someplace else."

Settler shrugged. Things were going well with the killing. It would be over soon. Maybe it was best to just let it play out, then get rid of the trapper.

"Let me think about it a while, Laura," Settler said and left the house.

Chapter 15

Three days after his conversation in the kitchen with his daughter, Jim Settler had an epiphany. It happened while he was alone in the drying shed looking at the stacks of wolf skins. The heads were still on them and he could see the horror in the dead eyes, a violent moment frozen in time. The jaws were half open and the tongues hung out as if they were thirsty. He heard a moan behind him and something caressed his shoulder. The rancher quickly turned to look. It was only the wind.

At that moment, getting rid of the wolves was no longer important. Laura had convinced him of that. The rancher was also worried about his men. Something could go wrong. Someone could get hurt. Bundy, Swift, Ford and Teller had already died. That was more than enough to bear, even though it wasn't his fault. They must have gotten careless. Hunter had mentioned the empty whiskey bottles found at the line shack.

When Gault, Hunter and Travis came back from the west sector that day, the rancher knew something had gone terribly wrong. He could see it by the expression on their faces.

"Where's Foley?" he asked, noticing Foley was missing.

Hunter and Travis avoided his stare as they dismounted, saying nothing. Gault spoke up as he climbed down from the buckboard. It was piled high with wolf pelts.

"Foley had a little accident," Gault said.

"What kind of little accident," Settler said flatly, with sarcasm.

"He accidently picked up a pellet of wolf's bane," Gault replied. "It slipped out of my hand and he picked it up."

Settler's face showed his disbelief and astonishment. "Hunter, what happened to Foley?" he said angrily.

Hunter nodded and said coldly, "It's like Mr. Gault said, Foley got careless and picked up one of the pellets. He shoulda known better."

Settler noticed Hunter no longer referred to him as boss, as he usually did. He wondered why. Did Hunter think he was working for Gault now, instead of him?

"Where's his body?" Settler asked. No one answered. "Where's his body?" the rancher repeated with a growl.

"We put it to good use," Gault said, cold as a stone.

"You what? You did what?"

"Like I said, we put it to good use," Gault repeated.

Settler now knew why Hunter and Travis had avoided his gaze. They had done a most despicable thing and they knew it and were ashamed of it. This foul deed would haunt them for the rest of their lives. It had disgraced them as cowboys. In fact, they were, by the code, no longer cowboys. They had forfeited their right to be called by that proud name.

The rancher glared at Gault. "Sir, you are finished here. I no longer require your services. I want you off my land and gone!"

"I'm not finished with my work here, Settler," Gault said, "the work you hired me to do."

"I've changed my mind," the rancher insisted. "Your services are no longer needed. I'll thank you to leave."

"I don't think I'll do that, Settler. I like it here. I like your men and your men like me as well."

Settler drew his gun and pointed it at Gault. "This is my land, Gault, and you are no longer welcome on it. So, get in your wagon and go."

"Hold it!" Hunter said. He and Travis drew their guns and pointed them at the rancher.

Settler glared at Hunter. His angry look quickly changed to sadness and pity. "Oh, Hunter! What has happened to you? And, you, too, Travis."

"Travis and me, we're with Mr. Gault now," Hunter said flatly. "We're going get revenge for Bundy, Swift, Ford and Teller. It seems like you forgot all about what the wolves did to them, Settler."

"You can't put the blame on me, Hunter! It was you who let them leave here drunk. You can't play stupid with the wolves. You know that."

"All I know is, I'm with Gault and he's going to clean every murdering wolf outta the west sector," Hunter said with a smirk on his face.

Gault turned to the rancher and said, "Settler, it's best you to go back into your house and stay there."

Settler was surprised. "Are you taking over my ranch, Mr. Gault?

"For now, yes," Gault said. "Travis, get his gun!"

Travis walked up to the rancher and took the gun from his hand. He carefully avoided his gaze. Settler looked over at Hunter, shook his head and then walked towards the ranch house.

"Stay in the house, Settler," Hunter said. "If you come out, it'll be bad for Miss Laura, if you get my drift. Don't force us to do anything we don't wanna do!"

Settler froze in mid-step. The muscles in his jaws rippled as he ground his teeth. He was about to answer angrily, but decided not to. Instead, he hurried across the yard and up across the porch. Moments later he was inside the house, in the kitchen.

"I saw and heard it all, Dad," Laura said. "What are we going to do?"

"Right now, I don't know."

"They can't get away with it, can they?"

"Gault holds all the cards right now. Hunter and Travis have sided with him."

"Poor Foley. What a horrible death it must have been for him. What they did to his body was horrible."

Toothless Mary was working over the stove. She seemed to be listening to every word. After she set out the meal of warmed up salted ham, pickled beets and mashed yellow turnips, she left quietly.

"I wonder what they'll do if Doctor Goodson comes out?" Settler asked.

"He won't be coming out for a while," Laura said. "He's gone back east to Chicago. His mother is ill."

"Oh, I'm sorry to hear that." Settler was pleased, but didn't let on. He thought about Tobey Nester. If he came out to the ranch, what would Hunter do to him? There could be trouble.

Chapter 16

The next morning Hunter rode out alone for the north sector. Late that evening five cowboys from the north sector rode in. As they pulled up in the yard, Settler and Laura came out on the porch to greet them. The cowboys quickly dismounted in front of the bunkhouse. They tied their mounts and started walking down to the mess tent.

"Jordan! Art Jordan!" Settler yelled across the yard at them.

Art Jordan, a tall, lean cowboy, separated from the group and approached the porch. He stopped a few feet away and saluted Laura.

"Good afternoon, Miss Laura," Jordan said.

"What are you doing in here, Jordan?" Settler asked. "You're supposed to be out at the north sector."

"I was, Mr. Settler, but Hunter came by an' asked some of us to come back in."

"What for?"

The cowboy looked uncomfortable. He stared down at the ground a moment before looking up at the porch.

"Well, Mr. Settler," Jordan said, "Hunter says we're gonna make a big move tomorrow ta clean out the wolves in the west sector, the ones thet killed Bundy, Swift, Ford and Teller. Bein' as me an' the boys were pals with them, we thought it only right thet we pitch in." Jordan paused for a moment, then said sheepishly, "Hunter said you ain't got the gall ta do it, Mr. Settler, so he's gonna see thet it's done."

"I'd rather you and the boys went back to the north line shack, Jordan."

"I can't do thet, sir. Hunter has given me an' the boys orders ta stay here."

"In that case, Jordan, you and the others are fired," Settler said with authority. He took a roll of money from his shirt pocket and peeled of some bills. He offered it down to the cowboy. "Here, take this. It a month's pay and more, for all of you. Now pack up and go."

Jordan shook his head. "Thanks, Mr. Settler," he said. "But we ain't leavin'. Hunter said Mr. Gault is gonna pay us double fer clearin' out the wolves."

"So, it's all about Mr. Gault's money, is it, Jordan?" Laura asked sharply.

"No, ma'am, Miss Laura, it's about revenge fer Bundy and the others, as I see it," Jordan replied respectfully.

"Where is Hunter now, Jordan?" Settler asked.

"He's a-ridin' fer the east line shack ta pick up a few more of the boys, sir."

With that, the cowboy turned and walked into the bunkhouse just as Gault was coming out. He saluted Laura.

"Mr. Gault, just what are you up to, sir?" she asked.

"It's very simple, ma'am," Gault replied. "Your father wants me gone, and I am going. But not before I set out all my traps. I have seventy-five of them. With that many traps and the poisoned meat we'll hang from the trees, it should put an end to the wolves in the west sector quickly and forever."

Laura glared hatefully at the trapper. Her father walked over and put an arm around her shoulders. Gault looked at her as if he were puzzled by her reaction to his words.

"What have we here, wolf lovers? It looks like we do. A rancher and his daughter who are wolf lovers? That's very strange indeed," Gault said. He shrugged and ambled over to his wagon, swinging his arms from side to side. From the rear, he looked like a small, hunched over gorilla.

Suddenly there was a commotion by the mess tent. Settler and Laura could see that Marty Parker was arguing with Travis.

"I ain't cookin' fer none a you sidewinders," Parker yelled.

Travis hit the old man hard in the face. The blow sent him down on his knees groaning and holding his left jaw.

"They're hurting Marty," Laura sobbed. "Can't you stop them, Dad?"

Settler rushed down off the porch and towards the mess tent. Travis saw him coming and turned to block him. He hit the rancher a blow to the stomach that knocked the wind out of him. Settler clutched his belly and knelt on the ground. The cowboy delivered another blow to the rancher's jaw that knocked him unconscious.

Travis pointed to two of the newly arrived men. "Carry him into the house."

They walked over to Settler, grabbed his arms and dragged him towards the porch. Laura followed them into the kitchen, and watched as they put her father in a chair. She knew both men by their names.

"Curt," she said, drying her eyes, "please help Dad and me."

Curt, the small, stocky one, looked away. "I ain't supposed ta talk to you, Miss Laura. I'm truly sorry."

She turned to the other one. "Phil?"

"Sorry, ma'am. Hunter is in charge now, an' Gault, too. They'll kill me if I don't follow orders."

Both men left and Toothless Mary came in carrying a pail of water. She put the pail down by the table and got a rag from the larder. Dipping it in the water, she stretched it over Settler's forehead. Laura wondered how she had gotten past the cowboys so easily.

Settler began to stir and gained consciousness. His jaw was bruised. "Are you alright, Dad?" Laura asked.

The rancher touched his jaw and nodded. They heard the sound of a horse riding into the yard. Laura hurried to the kitchen window and looked outside.

"Oh, no! It's Tobey Nester!" Laura cried. She ran into the hallway and opened the door to the porch. She had a clear view of the yard and watched anxiously as Travis confronted Tobey Nester.

"Whatta ya want here, Nester?" Travis asked scornfully.

"I come ta see Miss Laura, not thet it's any a yer business, Travis," Nester said as he slid down from his horse.

"Well, she ain't seein' nobody taday," Travis replied. "So, ride out."

"Says who?"

"Says me," Travis growled, stepping in front of Nester.

"Get outta my way, Travis!" Nester growled and brushed past the cowboy. He walked swiftly up on the porch and said, "Hi, Miss Laura."

"Turn an' face me, you stinkin' sodbuster!" Travis yelled.

Tobey Nester stopped on the porch a few feet from Laura. He turned slowly to glare back at Travis. Gault and the other cowboys were watching from the mess tent, waiting to see what was going to happen. It looked like a gun fight.

Just as Tobey Nester dropped his hand down by his gun, Travis drew and fanned off two shots into his chest at forty feet. The force of the bullets drove the young boy's body backward. Laura screamed as Tobey fell on his back in the hallway, groaning. She knelt by his side.

Her father came running from the kitchen. "Is he dead?"

"No, but he's in bad shape," Laura said gravely.

"Let's get him upstairs. Take his legs."

Settler grabbed Tobey under his arms and hoisted him upwards as Laura grabbed his legs. They struggled up the stairs and, after much effort, got him into the guest room and on the bed. Laura quickly got a towel, opened his shirt and pressed it against his wounds to stop the bleeding. Tobey looked up at her.

"Am I dyin'?" the young man whispered.

Laura forced a smile as she stared down into Tobey's face. "Shucks, no, Tobey, you're not dying. You'll be just fine."

"Well, thet's sure good ta know." Young Tobey Nester gave a big sigh. His head rolled sideways, and the light went out of his eyes. Laura's tears fell on his face. She knew he was dead.

A chorus of wolves started howling off in the distance in the hills behind the barn. Laura looked at her father. He put a hand on her shoulder. "You best go down to the kitchen. I'll be there shortly."

After she had left, Settler closed Tobey Nester's eyes and covered him with a blanket.

Chapter 17

Laura and her father sat in the kitchen staring at each other across the table. It was almost midnight, and they were emotionally drained as well as physically exhausted. From the sounds of things, the cowboys in the bunkhouse were drinking heavily as they waited for Hunter to come back from the east sector. The oil lamp on the table sputtered and flickered. Laura nodded. She was on the brink of dozing off.

"Go to bed, Laura," her father said. "You're tired."

"What are you going to do, Dad, stay up?"

"I can't sleep."

"Alright, I'll go lay on the bed."

Laura went up to her room. After she was gone, Settler rolled a cigarette and lit it. He sat back in his chair thinking about what he should do. Maybe it was best to just do nothing, just stay out of it. Gault said he'd leave when it was over and all the wolves were killed. He'd move on and kill more, someplace else. It looked like he was going to take Hunter and some of the boys with him.

Poor Tobey Nester. He was dead now. The cowboys would swear it was self-defense, fair and square. Gault would back them up. They were his men now. They would do anything he told them to do.

Settler heard horses pounding in the distance. He knew it was Hunter returning with men from the east sector. They'd ride out to the west sector early in the morning and kill all the wolves. Laura said there were about two hundred of them there. It would be a massacre, a complete extermination.

Hunter and three men from the east sector dismounted in the yard. The rancher could hear Hunter telling them to go down to the mess tent to get some food while he talked to Gault. Settler blew out the oil lamp, and he stood by the kitchen window in the darkness. He saw the glow of the light in the mess tent where Parker was still up cooking. Settler knew he must be tired and wished he could help him.

About half an hour later, the men from the east sector ambled up from the mess tent to the bunkhouse to join in the drinking. It seemed that Gault had a good supply of whiskey on hand. Settler could hear his guttural chuckle mixed with the voices of the cowboys. That pitiful, lonely thing was in there drinking along with the very men who would, in days to come, make jokes about his physical appearance. He would never be one of them, as much as he wanted to.

There would be no sleeping tonight. It would all be drinking and playing cards. A cowboy was never happier than when he was drunk or dancing with a painted lady and playing cards. Happy sounds came up from the bunkhouse. Someone played a harmonica and others sang along.

From his station in the dark by the kitchen window, Settler could hear a chorus of wolves howling behind the barn. It sounded like a call to assemble. He had heard that call before, over the years. He sighed and walked slowly into his study and got a shotgun from the gun cabinet. He loaded it, then filled his pockets with shells.

Taking the gun to the kitchen, Settler stood vigil at the window. He stood there in the dark staring out into the yard. The moon was bright except when banks of clouds drifted across its face to shut out its light. The talking, singing and laughing in the bunkhouse went on and on without stopping. Settler knew it would go on until dawn. Fights would break out. That's what usually happened when there was too much drinking.

The rancher yawned and was about to pull up a chair and sit down when he noticed movement out by the corral. Someone was opening the gate and letting the horses out. First one, then two, then all at once, they loped across the yard and into the field where Gault's wagon was anchored. They stopped to nibble on the dead grass, but suddenly gave a start and ran off. Either they had smelled danger or were threatened by something. Whatever it was, it had scared them enough to send them running.

Settler was fascinated by what he saw. His eyes caught the movement of a small, dark figure as it floated across the yard. It continued its slow, silent journey through the gate of the yard and across the road into the field. When it came to Gault's wagon it stopped and climbed into the back. It was inside quite a while and, when it came out, it dropped something on the ground and moved into the darkest shadows of the yard, out of sight.

Settler watched with interest as Gault came out of the bunkhouse. He seemed to be awfully drunk by the way his body weaved and wobbled. He muttered as he walked along, stutter-stepping erratically across the yard to his wagon. Once there, he heaved himself up inside, out of sight.

Settler's attention was suddenly drawn back to the bunkhouse. The door burst open and the cowboys came spilling out. Some carried whiskey bottles. One tossed a bottle high into the air, and another pulled his gun to shoot it but missed. Soon they were all firing drunkenly into the air. Hunter didn't seem as intoxicated as the rest and tried to get some control. From where he sat in a chair by the window, Settler counted over two dozen of them bunched up out there in the yard. It was too dark outside to see exactly who they were.

Hunter yelled, "Easy, boys, save some of them bullets for the wolves."

"Yeah, them rotten, stinkin', sneaky wolves," one cowboy hollered. "They killed Bundy. Bundy was my pal. So was Ford!"

Hunter turned and pointed at the house, bellowing, "And there he is, boys, the wolf lover, Jim Settler. Safe and sound in his bed. He's still alive while Bundy, Swift, Ford and Teller are all dead." He paused to see the effect of his words. The cowboys all stared quietly, almost soberly, at the ranch house, waiting for the words that would set them off like a stick of dynamite. The words came quickly.

"Whatta you gonna do about it, men?" Hunter shouted.

"Kill him!" someone yelled.

"Hang him!" another one joined in.

"Let's go!"

They started for the ranch house, an angry, drunken mob out for revenge.

Settler, quickly guessing their intention, grabbed the chair with one hand and ran into the hall. When he got to the door, he jammed it up under the handle. Turning quickly, he ran up to the second-floor landing with the shotgun, and stood staring down into the shadows of the hallway. Footsteps came pounding up on the porch. There was a loud bang, and the hallway door flew wide open.

Chapter 18

Laura heard the commotion and ran from her room. She saw her father on the second-floor landing. Walking quickly over, she stood beside him. Hunter stared up at them from down below. His body was framed in the opened hallway door, a threatening silhouette seen against the pale moonlight. The other cowboys stood out on the porch behind him, talking and drinking, waiting for his instructions. The howling of the wolves could be heard in the distance.

Hunter's voice boomed up at them. "Come on down, Settler!"

"I will if you promise to leave Laura alone, Hunter," the rancher yelled back at him. "Otherwise some of you are going to die this night!"

"Alright. No one will touch her," Hunter shouted back.

"Is that a cowboy's promise?"

"Sure. You got my word," Hunter replied. "It's you we're after, not her."

Settler looked at his daughter. She shook her head and said, "No, Dad, I can't let you do this. I couldn't live with myself if I did." She began to sob.

"We got no choice, girl. This is the best deal we're gonna get."

Hunter walked a few steps higher on the stairs and yelled, "What's it gonna be, Settler? Make it fast."

"Alright, I'm coming down," Settler said in a defeated voice. He leaned the shotgun against the railing, went to Laura and held her by the shoulders. "Don't cry, Honey. Don't give them that. You're a Settler. Stand tall. Show them what a Settler is made of."

The rancher turned away and walked slowly down the stairs. Laura felt the urge to cry. She choked it back and held it in as she watched Hunter follow her father to the bottom of the stairs. The big ramrod looked up at her, smirked, then turned to her father. "Outside, old man!"

The cowboys closed around Hunter and Settler as they made their way across the porch and into the middle of the yard. The ramrod brought them to a stop. Pointing to Jordan, he said, "Jordan, go get Gault. He'll wanna be in on this."

Hunter's eyes blazed insanely and his voice was strained with excitement.

Jordan laughed hysterically. "Sure, boss," he replied and ran off towards Gault's wagon. It was as if he was infected by some whiskey induced madness.

Settler looked around at his men. These weren't the cowboys he knew only a day or two ago. These men were strangers in the bodies of the men he used to know. The oddness of it sent cold chills of fear through him. He felt as if he had been thrust into the middle of a play written by some insane person. All he could do was watch helplessly as those around him performed their designated roles.

The wolves started to howl again, but much closer and louder this time. The sounds seemed to come from behind the corral, the barn and the bunkhouse. No one seemed to hear it except Settler.

Inside the house, Laura stood at the top of the stairs with her arms folded. She gazed towards the heavens as if seeking help. Her body shook as she sobbed. She looked downward at the emptiness below the stairs. The cowboys of the Rafter S were going to hang her father and she didn't know why, except that it seemed as if they had all lost their minds. That was the only thing she could think of.

Her thoughts were distracted as something moved in the darkness below. It came slowly up the stairs towards her. When it was halfway up, it stopped.

"Travis," she gasped in surprise.

"Hi, Miss Laura," the cowboy said. He stood staring at her, smirking with a crooked smile on his lips.

Laura stopped crying. "What do you want, Travis?"

"Just a little sugar is all, Miss Laura." Travis wasn't as drunk as the others. Evidently, he had been faking, waiting for the right moment to find her alone.

"Don't come up here!" Laura warned, wiping away her tears and clearing her eyes.

"Aw, now, be nice, Miss Laura. I ain't gonna hurt ya. A little lovin' is all I'm after."

"Please, Travis," Laura sobbed, "please go away."

Travis laughed, took another step, paused and then kept coming. He was near the top of the stairs when Laura grabbed the shotgun, aimed it at him, and pulled the trigger. The blast hit him in the chest, and the force of it sent him cartwheeling backwards through the air. His short, fast journey took him to the bottom of the stairs where he landed in a twisted, lifeless heap. Laura dropped the shotgun, covered her face with her hands and sobbed.

Out in the yard, the cowboys heard the shotgun go off and stared towards the house. "What was that?" one of them asked.

"It sounded like somebody fired a shotgun up in the house," another cowboy said.

"Forget it, we got somethin' more important to take care of," Hunter growled. He turned to Curt. "Go get a rope, Curt."

"Sure, boss," Curt said eagerly.

Curt was about to move out when Jordan came rushing out of Gault's wagon and down into the yard. He stumbled as he came through the gate, got up and began to vomit. Hunter and the other cowboys stared at him.

"What the hell got into yer craw, Jordan? Where's Gault?" Hunter asked.

Jordan blurted out in a sober voice, "He done met his maker!"

"What the heck are you talking about, Jordan?"

"Somebody poured some of them pellets right into his bed. Lordy, what an awful mess he is. All foamin' at the mouth and blood comin' outta his eye sockets an' ears! Oh, Lordy!" Jordan ran over by the bunkhouse, into the shadows and vomited again.

The wolves began howling once more, but no one paid any heed. The cowboys stood still as statues in the ranch yard, consumed by events of the moment. Hunter turned to Curt. "Go get that rope like I told ya, Curt. Hurry it up." Curt rushed away into the bunkhouse to get the rope.

Jim Settler faced Hunter and the others. "What did I ever do to you, Hunter, or the rest of you, that I deserve hanging?"

"Aw, shut yer trap, ol' man!" one of cowboys growled. His voice was sodden with drink. His eyes sparkled "We're gonna hang ya, burn yer house down, an' dance with Miss Laura." He laughed insanely.

Settler saw the hopelessness of his position. There was no way out. He heaved a sigh and nodded. "I guess Gault has turned you all against me, hasn't he? But he's dead now, so what sense does it make to kill me? It won't bring Bundy and the boys back to life."

At this point, they all became aware of the deep silence. The wolves had stopped howling.

"What's takin' Curt so long getting' thet rope?" someone asked in an edgy voice.

Over in the shadows by the bunkhouse, Jordan grunted, coughed, gasped and fell quiet. After that, it sounded like he was being dragged along the ground.

"What the hell's goin' on, Jordan?" a cowboy yelled out, "Hey, Jordan! You okay?" There was no reply.

The words were no more than out of the cowboy's mouth when Curt staggered out of the bunkhouse holding his throat with both hands. Blood gushed out between his fingers and ran down his arms. He tried to speak out, but only managed a gurgling sound. The others stared in horror as he fell forward on his face in the yard. His body thrashed around like a chicken with its head cut off. Finally, it came to rest.

"Wolves!" someone cried out. They all drew their guns.

"Oh, God! They're comin' fer us!" someone whined. "Just like they came for Bundy an' the boys!"

"Shut up that kinda talk!" Hunter cried out. There was a hint of panic in his voice. "Quick! Make a circle!"

The cowboys scrambled about, bumping into each other in confusion. Under Hunter's direction, they quickly formed a ragged circle facing outward, with their guns drawn. Hunter stood in the center, his Colt cocked and at the ready. He stared around the yard, squinting in the weak moonlight that filtered down through a bank of overhead clouds.

"Steady, men!" Hunter said huskily, trying to sound confident. It wasn't good enough to convince anyone, and he knew it.

Moments passed and a huge bank of clouds drifted across the face of the moon. It stalled there, casting the yard in blackness. There was the sound of movement, then grunts and gasps. When the sky cleared, there were three less men in the circle. One of the cowboys sobbed hysterically, and started firing wildly all around the yard. Others joined in and soon they were shooting in every direction until, finally, their guns were empty.

"Oh, God, no! Look! The clouds!" someone screamed in horror.

Another bank of clouds moved slowly across the face of the moon, and the yard went dark again. There was the thudding sound of impact and gurgling and gasping. When the moon came out, four more men were missing. Those left in the circle quickly began reloading their guns.

"Where's Settler?" someone yelled.

"He's gone!" another replied.

"Maybe the wolves got him!" still another yelled.

"I bet the skunk ran into the house!"

"I'm going after him," Hunter replied. He broke ranks and dashed for the porch.

With their ramrod gone, the rest were leaderless. "Head fer the corral," one terrified voice cried out.

Within seconds they were rushing down to the corral to get their mounts, only to find them missing. For the third time, a massive bank of clouds drifted over the moon again. They all stared up with looks of horror on their faces.

Up on the porch, Hunter took one last look at his cowboys, then ran into the hallway and slammed the door shut behind him. He looked down at Travis' body lying in a pool of blood. The ramrod stepped over it and walked to the foot of the stairs and stood in the shadows. Looking up, he caught a glimpse of Settler as he moved quickly away into the shadows on the upper landing. He fired a shot at him, but missed.

"There ain't no way out, Settler, so send her down!" Hunter yelled. He laughed as if he was drunk, insane or both. "Heck, I won't hurt her. I'll be gentle as a kitten."

"Go to the devil, Hunter!" Settler yelled down at him.

As he was about to fire again, Hunter heard heavy breathing close behind him. He felt a prickly sensation on the back of his neck. It grew warm and the hairs stood up. Whirling around, he fanned shots off in all directions until the hammer fell on an empty cylinder. He tried to reload but his fingers didn't work right, and he kept dropping the bullets on the floor. A low growling sound made him stop and look up.

Hunter whined as a huge black shadow fell over him. He smelled the stench of blood and raw flesh. The last thing Hunter saw were two green, iridescent eyes staring into his own. He tried to scream, but couldn't.

Chapter 19

Sunrise found Jim Settler and his daughter, Laura, barricaded in his bedroom. He had stayed awake all night, holding onto his shotgun, expecting the cowboys to come bursting in. But that never happened. Towards dawn, everything fell quiet.

Now that it was light enough to see, it seemed like a good time to check things out. The rancher shoved the bed away from the door and he and Laura walked down into the hallway. The floor was smeared with blood, but both Travis' and Hunter's bodies were gone. There were signs they had been dragged away.

Father and daughter walked out into the empty yard and looked around for signs of human life, but there were none. A few horses were at the water trough, and several more were walking down to the barn to hunt for grain. As for signs of human life, there were none.

A cold November wind blew small plumes of snow across the yard into the field. Far above them, in a cold, blue sky, buzzards circled on the wind currents.

Laura shivered. "They're all gone, Dad. Where did they go to?" she asked.

"The wolves took them," Settler replied wearily. "They dragged them off into the woods to share with the pack." He pointed upward. Huge, black birds flew in a circle above the hills to the west. "Looks like the buzzards are waiting for what's left over."

Laura began to cry. Her father put a hand around her shoulder to comfort her. "Gault started a war with the wolves, and it looks like the wolves fought back. Hunter and his men were stupid enough to go along, and they paid the price."

Laura finally got her crying under control and wiped her eyes. "Did you hear what Jordan said about Gault last night? About someone putting the poisoned pellets in his bed?"

"Yes, I heard."

"Who do you think would do such a thing?"

"It was Toothless Mary. She also released the horses from the corral."

"Are you sure, Dad?"

"I saw her do it."

They walked up to the yard gate and stared across the road into the field at Gault's prairie wagon. Laura pointed to something lying on the ground near the wagon. "Isn't that a bottle and a pair of gloves?"

Settler saw them and nodded. "Yeah. And the bottle is empty. Mary emptied the whole thing into Gault's bed." Settler started towards the wagon. "Stay here. I'll have a look."

"Be careful, Dad! Don't touch anything!"

The rancher walked up to the rear of the wagon and leaned over the tailgate and sniffed the air. He pulled back quickly and snorted, wiping his nose.

At that moment, Marty Parker came hobbling up from the chuck tent on bowed legs. Laura ran to him and gave him a hug. "Oh, Marty, you're alive!"

The old man laughed. "I sure am, Miss Laura, I sure am. When the shootin' started, I crawled up under the chuck wagon, inta the canvas sling where I keep the kindlin' wood."

Parker walked out into the field to join Jim Settler. The rancher was glad to see him and patted him on the back.

"I heard what Jordan said last night," Parker mused. "I reckon somebody didn't like Mr. Gault all that much."

"It looks that way, Marty," Settler said. "How do you think we should handle this?"

The old chuck wagon cook scratched his stubbly chin and sniffed the air. "If yer askin' me, I'd say the best thing ta do is give Mr. Gault a big sendoff."

"What kind?"

"The real hot kind. Set thet danged wagon a-fire, is what I'd do."

Settler gave the idea some thought then nodded. "Alright. Let's give Mr. Gault a proper burial, old friend. You take the oxen down to the water trough." He turned to Laura and said, "Honey, will ya go get a lamp. One with plenty of oil?"

"Sure, Dad."

As Parker went about rounding up the oxen, Laura hurried off into the kitchen. The rancher took off his bandana, and used it to pick up the bottle and gloves. He tossed them and the bandana into the wagon. Laura came back with the oil lamp and handed it to her father. He lit it and tossed it into the back of the wagon. It shattered with a bang and burst into flames.

In a few minutes, foul smelling smoke came curling out through the opening in the back end of the wagon. It was soon followed by flickering flames. The canvas covering began to bulge outward as the fire grew hotter. Tongues of red hot flames ate their way through the canvas and climbed upward towards the sky. The heat soon got so intense that Settler and Laura had to walk away.

Parker returned to stand alongside them. "I guess it's finished now, boss, ain't it?" Parker said.

"I sure hope it is, Marty," the rancher replied. "I hope and pray to God it is."

Toothless Mary smiled as she watched from the kitchen window.

Chapter 20

Jim Settler didn't know quite how to explain what had happened that night in the yard of the Rafter S Ranch. What could he say to make anyone believe him? There were two towns in the area. The farthest one was fifty miles north. The nearest one, Tall Pines, where the doctor and Toothless Mary lived, was where the cowboys went to get drunk and spend their money. It was only ten miles away to the east. The townsfolk would surely wonder why some of the Rafter S cowboys suddenly stopped coming in to drink and court the girls.

To be sure, those few cowboys still out at the north and east sectors knew the reason why some of their pals had ridden off with their ramrod, Hunter. They knew it was to wipe out the wolves of the west sector. How could Settler explain to them what had happened? Could he say they got crazy drunk and tried to hang him and that the wolves killed every one of them? Gault and Hunter had left him with a lot of explaining to do.

This was the dilemma Settler suddenly found himself in. He couldn't explain what happened that night, and yet he couldn't remain silent. People would eventually take notice and start asking questions.

There was only one hope, one saving factor, and that was Jim Settler's reputation and good name. Everyone knew the rancher was a righteous, God fearing man who had been a lynchpin in the community. He was known to be honest and true and he never turned his back on those in need of a helping hand. But, in telling the truth, he would make things worse for the wolves. Men would come from miles around with guns to wipe out the very wolves who had saved him and his daughter. And that would be a horrible tragedy.

Later that morning, Settler, Laura and Parker stood on the porch sipping coffee and watching Uriah Gault's wagon burn down to a pile of smoking ashes. After a while, Tobey Nester's father, Ty Nester, and the town marshal of Tall Pines came riding up. They stopped a moment to stare at the burning wagon, then rode into the yard and dismounted.

"Looks like somebody's wagon got burnt clean down to the rims, Jim. What happened?"

"Howdy, Marshal. Howdy, Ty," Settler said. He knew why Ty Nester was with Marshal Sanders. "It's a long story, Marshal." Then he said, "Ty, I suppose you're wondering why Tobey didn't come home last night."

"That's right, Jim," Ty Nester replied. "Is he here?"

The rancher looked down at his coffee cup, sighed deeply and shook his head. Ty Nester read the sign. The look on Laura's face said it, too. Old Marty Parker cleared his throat as if to make a speech.

"You got somethin' ta tell us, Marty?" the marshal asked.

"Well, Marshal, I reckon I might have."

"Well, spit it out, Marty," the marshal replied.

"I'll make it short an' sweet, Marshal. Norm Travis drew down on Tobey an' beat him to the draw."

"Why would he do thet?" the marshal asked.

"He never did like Tobey an' last night it came to a head. When Tobey came ta see Miss Laura, Travis had enough drinks in him ta pick a fight. An' thet's the beginnin' an' end of it, Marshal."

"Is that how it happened, Jim?" the marshal asked.

"That's how it happened, Marshal," the rancher said.

"Where's Travis?" the marshal asked. "I'd like to hear his side of the story."

Before Settler could answer, the old cook cut in. "He's gone, Marshal. Right after he kilt Tobey, Travis lit out like a scalded skunk. Took half the boys with him."

Settler was surprised by the false alibi offered by the old man. He was going to correct it, but the marshal interrupted him with, "Where's Hunter, Jim?"

Settler heard himself saying, "After Travis left, I fired him. I blamed him for not stopping the fight."

The marshal closely watched Settler's eyes as he spoke. Finally, he nodded and said. "I guess he had it comin'." The marshal then looked in the direction of the burnt down wagon. "What the story on that?"

After that first lie, the second lie came easier for the rancher. "Some trapper stopped over there in the field. His name was Gault. He asked if I had any pests that needed taking care of. He spent a few days here talking with the boys and doing some drinking. Strange but nice fellow. Seems like he set himself on fire, by the looks of it. Most likely got drunk and turned over a lamp. It must have happened just before sunrise."

Ty Nester got the question off his chest. "Where's Tobey?" he asked, biting his lips to keep from sobbing.

"Up in the house, Ty," Settler replied. "His horse is in the corral. You can use my buckboard."

"Thanks, Jim."

"Would you two like to come in for coffee?"

"Thank you, Jim. Sure," Nester replied. The marshal nodded in agreement.

As they walked across the yard to the porch, Parker hustled down to the barn to hitch up the small buckboard. Ty Nester came alongside Laura and caught her attention.

"Tobey really liked you, Miss Laura. I guess you know that."

Laura nodded and replied, "I liked him a lot, too, Mr. Nester."

When they went into the kitchen, Laura saw that Toothless Mary had placed a blackberry tart on the table. A fresh pot of coffee was steaming on the stove.

Chapter 21

It was a long, cold, dreary winter and the snow was deep. Settler gave his new men a lecture, telling them that they were hired to wrangle cows, not to hunt wolves. Hardly anyone ever saw the wolves, and, when that happened, it was at a great distance. Not chasing down wolves made it easier for the cowboys since it allowed them more time for playing cards and sleeping.

As for the wolves, they were practically invisible and took down mostly the old and lame cows and the strays that wandered away from the main herd. That was enough to feed the pack. They knew they were no match for the bulls and stayed well out of their way.

It was springtime when Laura received a letter from Doctor Tom Goodson. He wrote to tell her that he wanted to marry her. She wrote back saying she would consider his proposal, but would hold off until he offered it in person. He soon answered that his mother had passed away after her long illness. Now that the funeral was over, he would take a train to Tall Pines. He asked her to meet him at the station.

Laura arrived at the depot on the appointed day and time. When the passengers got off, Goodson was not among them. Since the next train wasn't due until the following day, she decided to return to the ranch. Just as she was leaving, Marshal Sanders came rushing out of the telegraph office. He hollered and approached her with a piece of paper in his hand.

"Hello, Marshal Sanders," Laura said, staring at the telegram.

"I'm glad I caught you," the marshal said. "I was just about to ride out to the ranch."

"Oh? What about, Marshal?"

"It's about Doctor Goodson," the marshal replied. He sighed, looking uneasy. "Maybe we should talk over at the jail."

Laura's heart began to beat faster. "Did something happen to him?" she asked.

"Yes. I just got a wire from the marshal in Ellsworth. The doctor was hurt badly in a train robbery on the way from Kansas City. Before he died, he managed to tell the railroad police about his office in Tall Pines and about getting word to you... that he loved you. It's all here, in the telegram, if you want to read it."

Laura looked away for a moment, then said sadly, "Yes."

The marshal handed her the telegraph. She read it with tears in her eyes and finally stuck it in her jacket pocket. "Thank you, Marshal."

"Are you alright? Is there anything I can do, Miss Laura?"

"No, Marshal," Laura replied, avoiding the marshal's sad look. "Come see us when you get a chance."

Holding in her sorrow and grief, she returned to the Rafter S with a heavy heart.

. . .

In mid-spring, Laura felt the urge to get away from the ranch and all its responsibilities. She put on her riding habit and packed some jerky and hardtack in a saddlebag. Strapping on her gun, she mounted up and rode out, heading west. It was early, and she was in no hurry. The warm, fresh air was invigorating. The scent of nature awakening and growing after a long rest was everywhere. The sky was blue and filled with cottony clouds. Birds flew in flocks, their calls filling the air. She rode slowly.

After a time, Laura found herself by a small, grassy glade near a stream. The branches of the pines slanted over, closing it in shadow. Somehow it seemed familiar. She stopped, dismounted, and tied her horse to a pine tree. Getting the saddlebags, she walked to the stream. Once there, she set them down and knelt to drink. It was cool and refreshing.

Laura ate a bit of food and lay back to listen to the sounds of nature. Chipmunks chattered in the brush. Blue jays played in the trees. She soon dozed off into a half-dream like state. It was then she seemed to hear a familiar voice her mind.

"You have come back, *Nee-lah-sol-lah*," it said.

She heard her own vice answer, "Yes, *Shu-dah-gay-lah*. I've come to thank you for saving me and my other father, the human one."

"You are my daughter. What else could I do?"

"How did you know I was in danger?"

"*Suh-lah-mah-dee*, the old Comanche woman, told me. She mind-speaks with our kind."

"She is like a mother to me. I am keeping her close. Where is the old Grey One who marked me?"

"He has taken his journey to the spirit world."

"I am sorry to hear of that."

"It is a journey we all must take someday."

"Lay by my side," she heard her mind-voice say. "Be with me a while, Father."

"I will always be with you, little *Nee-lah-sol-lah.* I will be as your guardian spirit, even after I have gone from this place to the spirit world."

Laura found his words comforting.

The big, black wolf came into the cool shadows and lay down by Laura's side.

The End

Western books by R. Annan

Fight for the Lazy M
The Red Bandana
The Salvation of Trace Logan
The Cowboy from Sierra Blanca

Jack Cordell Westerns

The Gunfighter in Winter
Long Ride to Hell's Kitchen
Owl Hawks
Gunfight at Barfield Springs
Shootout at Sanctuary City
Last Days of a Gunfighter

Clay Jared Westerns

Copperhead Moon
Cowboys of the Box R
Prisoners of Brimstone Pass
Range War in C Minor
Devil Wind
Showdown at Wamego Falls
Lightning Riders
Winter Kill
Wild River
Shootout at Rattlesnake Flats

Jesse Garnett Westerns

Gunfight at Black Wolf Lair
Gunfight at Latigo Junction
Outcasts of Troublesome Creek
Stagecoach at Bremer's Rock

About the Author

As a young boy growing up in the city, R. Annan never passed up a chance to see a western movie. His heroes were Buck Jones, Johnny Mack Brown, Wild Bill Elliot and John Wayne, to name a few. As an adult, he often wondered where his love of westerns came from. Perhaps it has something to do with his grandfather, John L. Annan, who was a cowboy from Helena, Montana, in days of old.

R. Annan is a seasoned and traveled author with many interests. As a career serviceman, he served in Korea and Vietnam. He also completed a one-year course at the Defense Language Institute at Monterey, California, and graduated from the University of South Florida with a B.A. in Art and Art History. After taking a two-year course in screenwriting at the Hollywood Scriptwriting Institute, he established The Old Time Radio Club Time Machine as both a scriptwriter and an actor.

A Note from the Author

Thank you for reading my book. If you enjoyed it, would you please consider rating and reviewing it? I'd enjoy your feedback. Thank you!